"An important and hopeful book about the power of God's love in healing the broken."
—*Richard Paul Evans, #1 New York Times Bestselling Author*

"*Shattered Innocence* is a gripping story of a young girl kidnapped and forced into sexual slavery. It is also a mandate to get involved in helping the many innocent, abused children caught up in the horrors of human trafficking. As the author of a fiction series on this topic, I've heard from a handful of trafficking survivors how grateful they are for anyone who helps get the word out about the reality of this horrific crime, so more people can get involved and help fight this in every way possible."
—*Kathi Macias, bestselling award-winning author of more than fifty books, including* Deliver Me From Evil

"*Shattered Innocence* reminds us that the journey to freedom can be arduous with many turns, but God's faithfulness abounds. Author Dejah Edwards gives us a front row seat, as she masterfully navigates the reader through this journey to freedom."
—*Pastor Tom Villalobos, Oak Valley Church, Yucaipa, CA*

"As I read Dejah Edwards' book, *Shattered Innocence...A Journey to Restoration,* I was once again reminded of the power of God to heal a damaged soul. Dejah weaves together the story of a life that was broken, yet miraculously put back together and then ultimately used to restore others. Your faith will be lifted as you read this book and know that God is able to make even the tragic turns of our life work towards His purpose."
—*Pastor Bryan & Cynthia Rosenbarger, Grace Chapel, Loxahatchee, FL*

"Dejah Edwards not only has a heart for woman, but is the woman that knows the heart of a woman. Speaking to the heart of a woman comes easy to Dejah because the measure of her strength comes from her picking up her shattered pieces. Her courage, confidence, resilience, and relentless determination to live have carved a path

for many other women to follow. Dejah's voice truly echoes hope, strength, peace, joy, and most importantly, faith. Her heart knows the language of love, and you will experience love as you journey through this book, *Shattered Innocence...A Journey to Restoration.*"
—*Michele DeCaul, Life Coach and Author, Orlando, FL*

"Dejah Edwards has eloquently woven the challenges of overcoming the trauma that sex exploitation victims will deal with for the rest of their lives. There are important lessons intertwined in a riveting story of a young girl who becomes the victim of sexual trafficking and subsequently tries to start her life over as if nothing had happened. This book is a must read for anyone who has experienced personal trauma (emotional or physical) and is trying to deal with 'life as usual.' Shame and trauma are life-changing events that only the generosity and grace of God can heal. All of us must acknowledge the pain and hurt in our lives if we are to find the freedom of self acceptance. Congratulations to Dejah Edwards on creating a story that is powerful and intriguing and is sure to change the lives of the readers."
—*Opal Singleton, President and CEO Million Kids, Instructor University of Southern California, Radio Host:* "Exploited: Crimes Against Humanity" and "Exploited: Crimes and Technology"; *Author of* Seduced: The Grooming of America's Teenagers and Societal Shift: A World without Borders, A Home without Walls

Shattered Innocence

A Journey to Restoration

A Novel

Dejah Edwards

RIVER BIRCH PRESS

Daphne, Alabama

To Ron—
You are my greatest
adventure

Contents

Acknowledgments

Much appreciation and thanks to:

My husband, Ron, God's gift to me.

My dear friend Lori Nichols, my first reader and who cheered me on to completion.

Larry J. Leech II, my first editor, who challenged and encouraged me.

Jennifer Gates, whose prayers and support I cherish.

Kathi Macias, my second editor, for her invaluable help and gracious sweet spirit.

Cheryl Ricker for her faith in me and for always believing in my book.

My Lord and Savior, Jesus Christ, who heals and restores.

"You may choose to look
the other way,
but you can never say again
you did not know."

—*William Wilberforce*

☞ 1 ☜

The Escape

Move, Lyndie! This is your way out.
I glanced down at the blood dripping down my forearm. It didn't matter how I'd cut myself. That was the least of my worries. *Oh, God, please help me!*
It took every ounce of my strength to pry open the gas station window and then squeeze my small body past its jagged edges. I didn't know what to expect on the other side of the window, but it couldn't be as horrific as what was behind me. Birthing through the narrow window, I dropped about six feet onto my right shoulder and head, rolling sideways onto the ridged metal bed of an old flatbed truck.

I was so filled with fear and adrenaline that I hardly noticed the pain of my fall as I scrambled under a heavy blue tarp to the farthest section of the truck's bed. I hid myself in a musty wooden crate scattered with a small pile of rotten corn.

The minutes felt like hours. *How long would I be here?* I knew Hank. He would find the open window and would be out after me soon, like a man frantically looking for his lost wallet. Suddenly, the truck's engine grumbled to life. The entire truck shivered as it fired up. *Was I really escaping this five-year nightmare?*

The corn's crisp, earthy smell filled my nostrils as the truck lurched forward. It stopped again at the edge of the highway, then pulled out onto the highway, rocking me back and forth with its motion. *Was this really happening? Was I really free?*

Suddenly a car pulled up beside the old truck. I pressed myself to the back of the crate, wishing I could be invisible. *Please*

1

don't let it be him. The car held in formation for only a moment, then sped past us.

Maybe ten minutes later the truck slowed and turned off the highway onto a bumpy dirt road. I felt my body relax. A full half an hour passed before the truck rattled to a stop. *What now?* The door opened and the driver got out. I slowly squeezed myself out of the crate to peek under the tarp, but I couldn't see anybody. Suddenly a large golden retriever raced toward me, barking wildly. I tucked myself back into the crate and held my breath.

The truck door creaked open. "What's up, girl?" a man's voice said. "C'mon, let's get some breakfast."

The dog kept barking.

"C'mon, girl. You heard me. Let's go in and get some breakfast."

The dog looked back and forth between us, then followed the man. The screen door slammed behind them. I stayed in the crate, unsure what to do next. I hadn't thought where I was going, only what I was running from. *What next?*

A few minutes later the smell of bacon awakened my senses. I couldn't remember the last time I'd eaten. The pain from my escape started to manifest—a sharp aching in my side, a bump on my head, the cut on my arm. I was wiping the blood from my arm onto my pants when I heard the dog barking nearby again. She jumped and scratched her claws against the metal sides of the flatbed.

"What's got you so riled, girl?" the old man said. Gravel crunched beneath his feet as he made his way over. He stopped a few yards from my side of the truck. I could hardly breathe. "What you find, girl?"

He yanked off the tarp, and our eyes met. For a moment we just stared at one another. I saw him glance at the blood on my arm. "Well, lookie here. We have a stowaway. Hello, Miss."

I shrunk back in the crate for safety.

"It's okay. I won't hurt you. Let's get you outta there." He reached out to give me a hand. I closed my eyes. Over the last five years I had been in many men's hands. I'd learned to disassociate myself from their touch. Except this man's touch was different somehow. Gentle. His strong steady arms gently lifted me from my nesting place, setting me on the ground.

"My name's Sam," he said. "My dog here's Sandy. Who might you be, young lady?"

My heart beat so loud, I was sure both the man and dog could hear it.

Hank will kill me, kept going through my mind. *Did he know Hank? Had this man raped me?*

The grandfatherly man looked to be in his sixties. I wanted to run, but where would I go? Besides, I wouldn't get far. I was too weak.

"You look starved. Let's get you something to eat." He gently smiled. "Maybe you'll feel more like talkin' with a full stomach. That's how I am. C'mon in."

I just stood there.

"C'mon, I'm not going to hurt you. I know you're hungry."

I don't know how he knew, but I was. The smell of the bacon still lingered. I craved it.

"This way." He turned his back and started toward the house. I glanced behind me, then slowly followed after him.

2

The Farmhouse

I collapsed into a wooden chair at a long barn kitchen table that looked like it had been handcrafted. Sam lived in a small, modest home. A wood-burning stove stood in one corner, a drop-leaf table with an antique flowery vase in the other. Next to the vase stood a silver frame with a picture of a pretty woman with loving eyes.

Sam scooped bacon, eggs, biscuits, homemade jam, and baked apples onto my plate. I was about to dig in when Sam bowed his head. "Lord, we thank You for this nourishing food for our bodies. And thank You for bringing us this new friend. In Jesus' name, amen."

His broad, strong, rugged shoulders reminded me of an older kind of lumberjack. He had weathered skin, probably from working outside. His sandy brown hair had a touch of gray at the temples. Must have been at least six feet tall. His eyes were deep-set blue, radiating care and tenderness. It seemed he could see inside my soul.

I ate quickly, grateful he didn't immediately press me to talk. Sandy, with her thick fur and massive paws, kept her head on my lap.

"Seems you found a new friend, Sandy." Sam looked at me. "Well, Missy, we have lots of food here, so you don't need to worry. You're safe with us."

Safe. I couldn't help myself. I burst into tears and jumped up from the table.

"Sorry," I said, running out the front door. "I gotta go."

I kept running until I reached the corral where I spotted a

beautiful horse. Slowly, cautiously, I nudged closer to the animal. Her big brown eyes studied me while I gently stroked her head. What a calming feeling to touch this massive beast.

Sandy managed to catch up with me, wagging her tail, nudging me with her wet nose. Sam caught up to us both.

"Honey," he whispered. "We mean you no harm. You're welcome to stay with us as long as you like. We just want to help. Will you kindly let us lead you back to the house where you can freshen up and get comfortable? You'll probably want a bath and some good rest."

"Do I really smell that bad?"

Sam laughed. "Of course not."

Lacking a better plan, I followed him and Sandy back to the farmhouse.

Back in the kitchen, he returned with a pink basket, carrying everything a girl would want—bubble bath, shampoo, sweet smelling lavender soap, lotion, and a pink, fluffy thing for washing. Folded over his arm was a delicate pink flannel robe, a pink nightgown, and pink bedroom slippers.

"These here things belonged to my Sarah. She was a tiny little thing, like you."

I wanted to ask Sam if Sarah was the lady in the picture frame, but I didn't yet feel comfortable enough to pry.

A warm bath turned out to be just what I needed. I lay back and let myself melt into it. *When was the last time I'd had a bath?* It had been years. Hank and Carol only let me take periodic showers—and they were cold ones. Mostly they just pointed me in the direction of a bucket and commanded, "Wash yourself up." Unlike Hank's scratchy old towels, Sam's towels were big, soft, fresh—and pink. Like the nightclothes he gave me to wear.

Sam's voice called through the door. "There's a new toothbrush and a tube of toothpaste in the medicine cabinet. Oh, and there's also a brush and comb in the right-hand drawer. I've gotta do chores, but I'll see you in the morning. Hope you can get some rest."

After a few more wonderful minutes, I climbed out of the tub and opened the drawer. I reached for the brush and comb—both pink. I needed to ask Sam about this pink thing.

When I got to the bedroom, I felt fresh as I put on the soft nightgown. And what a feeling to lay down on a bed. For the first time in years, I found myself able to relax. And then, I just slowly let myself drift away...

"Wake up, missy. You're okay. You're here with us now. No one can hurt you."

I rubbed my eyes and looked up into Sam's kind face and then at his faithful dog by his side. Oh, my goodness. My face and pillow felt all wet.

"Missy, you were screaming and crying."

"Oh, I'm so sorry," I said. "I didn't mean to wake you."

"Don't worry about it. Why don't I bring you some warm milk to help you get back to sleep? Wait, I know. Do you think some chocolate chip cookies would help too?"

I smiled and nodded. I thought about how chocolate chip cookies were both my dad's and my favorite. Mom and I used to make them for him when he came back from government business trips.

The warm milk turned out to be just what I needed to fall back to sleep.

When I finally got out of bed late the next day, the nightmare came back full force—a detail-packed nightmare where Hank and Carol had found me and taken me back. *Really, what could be scarier?* It felt so real. And they'd abused me severely for running away.

Unable to shake it, I cried most of the day. Sam left me alone until it was almost suppertime.

"Honey, I have a pot roast cooking in the crockpot. How's about I bring you some when it's done?"

"Thanks a lot, Sam."

I stayed in bed for the next three days, alternately crying and sleeping. I guess I was more exhausted than I thought. Sam was kind enough to leave me alone and only come around to give me something to eat. When Sandy whimpered at the door, Sam would chase her away. By the time the third night rolled around, Sandy slipped into my room.

"No, Sandy," Sam scolded. "Leave her alone. She needs her rest."

"It's all right," I said. "She can stay. In fact, I'd like that." I petted the dog, and she immediately jumped on the bed, nestling close. She was true to the breed—friendly, tolerant, and intelligent.

The next morning, Sandy scratched at the door, wanting out of my room. When I cracked open the door, a delicious aroma filled my nostrils. Sam whistled a vaguely familiar tune in the kitchen, and I decided to join him there.

"Well, look who's here." Sam smiled at me. "Good morning, Missy, It's a mighty fine morning. I just made some French toast and squeezed some fresh orange juice. Want some?"

"Yes, please." When I sat, Sam bowed his head. "Thank you, God, for a glorious new day. Thank You for our new friend, and please help heal her heart."

Tears filled my eyes, and Sam must have noticed before blurting, "Want to help me feed the animals this morning?"

I nodded, excited at the thought of meeting the animals.

After we finished breakfast, I followed Sam outside. Sandy stayed close and licked my hand every chance she got.

I'd never been in a barn before. What a treat to step in. Horses, cows, pigs, chickens, and a pony. He had it all. And each had its own distinct character and smell.

Sam dropped some hay in my hand and gently showed me how to offer it to the horses and pony. Stroking the beautiful creatures, I was amazed at how friendly they were.

While milking a cow, Sam called over to me, "That there horse is Daisy. How'd you like to take a ride on her later?" Daisy was the horse I'd poured my heart out to the day of my arrival on the farm.

I smiled but didn't answer. I just sat on a low bench and threw feed out to the chickens. They tickled my skin as they pecked at my toes.

Sam gathered eggs from the hens while Sandy herded a stray pig back into his pen. The sun was high in the sky when we finished feeding the animals.

He thrust a basket in my hand and whispered, "Let's go pick blackberries. We can put them in the homemade ice cream I'm making for tonight's dessert."

We picked dozens of berries, but we ended up eating more than we put in our baskets. After over an hour of fun, we headed back to the house.

I went into the bathroom and looked in the mirror. Ah! My face was nearly as blue as my berry-stained hands. I laughed out loud, something I hadn't done in years, and it felt good.

"Lunch is ready!" called Sam.

I sat at the table and Sandy licked my hand, her head resting on my lap. As he did at every meal, Sam bowed his head and thanked God for our food, his animals, and me.

My eyes grew wide as he set down in front of me the largest loaded turkey sandwich I'd ever seen. I shook my head as I looked at the lettuce, tomato, and cheese sticking out of it alongside the potato salad and plump dill pickle.

"Sam, the meals you've prepared are wonderful. It's amazing to have all this delicious food. I haven't eaten like this in years." My captors nearly starved me. In their house, I was lucky to eat once a day, and, sometimes, nothing more than scrapes and water.

Sam looked at me with eyes of compassion. "Save some room for my homemade apple pie."

After we cleared the table, Sam looked at me and smiled. "Well, Missy, now ... the highlight of your day. Let's go saddle up Daisy and Rocket and take an afternoon ride."

With both excitement and apprehension, I followed Sam to the barn. Sandy stayed by my side every step of the way. In a short amount of time, I'd come to trust this man. There was something different about him. For one thing, he was the exact opposite of my kidnapper, who had been all things insensitive and cruel. All Hank ever did was hurt me. Sam, on the other hand, showed me nothing but kindness and love. He clearly wanted to help me. Being with him reminded me of the feeling I had when I was with my dear, sweet grandmother too many years ago to count.

Sam taught me how to brush Daisy, which I happily did as he saddled Rocket. After he saddled both horses, those same strong and gentle arms that had lifted me from the flatbed truck now lifted me up to the saddle. He taught me to give Daisy a slight kick. When I did, I suddenly felt a sort of freedom. As we trotted down the path, the wind blew through my hair.

As we rode, Sam sang a song I vaguely remembered my grandmother singing. It was the same tune he'd whistled a few days ago—"Amazing Grace."

I took a deep breath and inhaled the sharp fragrance of wildflowers and trees, wishing I could ride like this forever. Before long, a misty rain sprinkled down. It didn't faze me at all. I closed my eyes, imagining we were heading off into a faraway land with castles and princes.

"Lookie there, Missy." Sam's words startled me out of my daydream.

He pointed at the sky, and I gasped at the most brilliant rainbow I'd ever seen. "God's promise." The words flew out of my mouth before I thought about what I was saying.

"You're right, Missy. God put the bow in the sky to remind us of his promise never to destroy the earth by water again."

My mind wandered back to when I was a little girl in my bedroom back home. I remembered noticing my favorite book on the shelf. "Read this one, Mama," I said. *Noah and the Rainbow.* Just then, tears trickled down my face. My mother. My heart ached for her.

"It's getting late," said Sam, probably detecting my sadness. "Time to head home for ice cream." I licked my lips.

An hour later, we returned to the farm. I helped Sam wipe down the horses and feed them hay. He grabbed the fresh eggs the hens laid, and we headed for the house.

"Want to smash the blackberries while I put together the ice cream?" he asked.

That's when it struck me. Sam had taken me on the trail ride, not just for an adventure, but to help me heal. I looked into his eyes. "Yes, I'd like that a lot. Um, Sam?"

"Yes?"

"My name is Lyndie. Just so you know."

Sam petted Sandy. "Your new friend's name is Lyndie." She barked and offered me her paw. I laughed for the second time today.

As we shared the scrumptious meal, I finally got the nerve to ask what I'd been wondering about. "Is that Sarah's picture in the kitchen, next to the vase of wildflowers?"

He nodded, a slight distant look in his blue eyes. "Yes, she was my darling, my high school sweetheart. Married her when I came home from the war in Vietnam. We were married for over thirty years." His shoulders slumped. "The short story of it is— she got sick with pneumonia and died. She's been gone nearly five years now."

I waited a moment, then asked, "Was her favorite color pink?"

Sam chuckled. "How'd you know?"

I smiled. "Please let me clean up," I said. "You go relax."

After finishing in the kitchen, I joined him in the living

room. Combined smells from his pipe and hickory logs in the wood-burning stove filled the room. I dropped onto the couch, and wouldn't you know it, Sandy came over and lay at my feet.

Even as Sam smiled, his eyes still held a slight faraway look. "She used to do the same thing with my Sarah. Guess she misses her as much as I do." He stood up and patted Sandy, then walked toward the kitchen. "The ice cream should be just about ready."

Minutes later, he came back with a couple of full bowls. I took one bite and smacked my lips. "This is the best ice cream I ever tasted."

Sam chuckled. "Tomorrow we need to run into town." He took a quick bite. "We'll get you some clothes and other things you're going to need while you're here with us."

Fear gripped my heart. *What if they're looking for me?* I wanted to tell him why I couldn't go, but I didn't want to ruin the moment. I'd tell him tomorrow, I decided.

Sam set down his empty bowl and snatched a Bible from the coffee table. "I'd like to read to you from my favorite book, Lyndie. It gave me a lot of comfort when I lost my Sarah. And it still feeds me now."

He propped the Bible open on his lap, and I listened to him read from the book of Genesis. I remember getting groggy. The last thing I remember before, half-asleep, I felt his strong arms lifting me up, taking me to my bed and covering me with a pink blanket. *Why did I feel only peace with this man?* Usually when men carried me into a bedroom, they were rough. Fear would claw through me like a premonition because I knew what they would take from me.

A wet snout tapping my face told me it was morning and time to get up. "Stop, stop, Sandy." I laughed as she jumped onto the bed and full-fledged licked my face.

"You up, Lyndie?" Sam's voice called from the kitchen.

"Got blackberry pancakes with my own homemade butter."

I lunged out of bed and raced to the kitchen. "Wow, pancakes. Yummy!"

Sam set down a plate and poured melted butter and hot maple syrup on top. My dad used to make me animal and Mickey Mouse shaped pancakes. Oh, how I missed him and his embrace and the smell of the cologne he wore.

Sam put his hand on mine as he sat down. This time I knew enough to hold off on eating until he prayed. I bowed my head as he did, and I listened, fascinated with each word.

"Lord, thank you for this glorious day. Thank You for my health and my home. Thank you for Lyndie. Help heal her heart and take away her pain."

Before Sam could say another word, I blurted it out. "I can't go to town. And please don't ask me to tell you why. I can't tell you just yet."

The look in his eyes told me he understood. "Whatever you say. I'll just check the sizes on the clothes you came in, so I know what to buy for you."

Relief washed over me. "Thanks." Thank goodness he didn't press me to explain. I wasn't ready to disclose everything or anything. At least not now, anyway.

3

Kidnapped

Sam scanned me carefully. "You wear about a size six shoe, right?"

I nodded, surprised at his accuracy.

"While I'm gone, you'll be safe with Sandy. In your bedroom, you'll find clothes that belonged to my sweetheart. Wear whatever suits you. And if you don't mind, could you please start feeding the animals? I'll be back as soon as I can."

A smile spread across my face. "Of course, I will. I'd love to. I'll clean up the dishes too."

He returned my smile. "Thanks a bunch."

As I tried on the clothes, Sandy didn't take her eyes off me. She laid her head on one of Sarah's blouses.

"You miss her too, don't you, girl?"

She barked.

"I understand. I miss my family too. I want to go home so bad—but I can't. They'd be ashamed of me."

Pushing the thought aside, I slipped into a pair of denim overalls and a pink Henley shirt. Sarah's clothes were a little big, but nothing a little roll up of the pant legs and shirtsleeves couldn't fix. "Sandy, I wish I was as pretty as Sarah."

The dog followed me out to the barn and watched me lay my head on Daisy's neck. "I love you too," I whispered into her ear.

Sandy ran back and forth, following me closely from animal to animal as I fed them. She really thought she was helping me. What a trip!

After I finished feeding the pigs, Sam pulled up in his truck.

13

He gave a little horn honk, and Sandy ran to him. His arms quickly filled with packages, and I noticed more in the truck. I stared in astonishment with my mouth wide open at all his purchases. He chuckled at me. "Yeah, I guess I went a little overboard. But our girl needs a wardrobe, doesn't she, Sandy?"

Sandy barked.

"Come on. Let's go into the house to see how you like your new duds."

Sam seemed to enjoy giving me clothes even more than I enjoyed receiving them. There were two pairs of jeans, two flannel shirts, a pink hoodie sweatshirt, four blouses, underwear, socks, and sneakers. He also had bought a comb, brush, lotion, powder, and a small suitcase. But those things weren't the best of it all. Seeing a box of assorted chocolates, I let out a squeal.

"And, of course, I didn't forget Sandy." He pulled out some doggie treats, which she gobbled up, as I stared at all his purchases.

Grateful beyond words, I threw my arms around him. I hadn't hugged anybody like that in a long time, and it felt warm and comfy like when I hugged my grandma.

Over the next few weeks of my stay, I played with Sandy, fed the animals, rode Daisy, and gobbled down fabulous meals like some kind of a queen. But what I looked forward to most was Sam's after dinner Bible reading. The words written in the book truly brought comfort and hope. I learned more and more about Jesus and how He loves me.

One night, after reading from the book of Revelation, Sam got quiet. He looked at me seriously. "Do you want to go there?"

I frowned. "Where?'

"Heaven. That'll be our eternal home. Our time on this earth is short. We're just passing through. Heaven is forever, and there's no pain there, no hurt. No tears either."

I broke into sobs. No more pain. I couldn't imagine a place

without it. But there was no pain with Sam, only peace. *What secret did this man have?*

He moved from the rocker onto the couch by me. Gently, he put his right hand around my shoulder. I kept smothering tears on my sleeves. I finally felt like I belonged somewhere. I let my body rest against him. I let him hold me while I cried.

When I got all the sobs out, Sam looked at me tenderly. "Lyndie, I know you've suffered greatly. Some horrible things have happened to you by some mean-spirited people who clearly hurt you deeply. But you can't keep this inside forever. You must let it go, give it to the one who suffered and died for you...the one who took all your hurt and pain upon himself on the cross. The Bible says, 'Surely he took up our pain and bore our suffering.' I need to ask you: Would you like his peace and joy in your life? Would you like the assurance of eternal salvation and know for sure you'll go to heaven someday, never to suffer or cry again? Would you like to give your heart to Jesus right now—tonight?"

I nodded. "Yes! Oh, Sam, yes!"

Sam led me in a simple prayer. "Dear Lord Jesus, I know I'm a sinner, and I ask for Your forgiveness. I believe You died for my sins and rose from the dead. I trust and follow You as my Lord and Savior. Guide my life and help me do Your will. In Your name, amen."

With eyes closed I repeated the prayer after him. Immediately I felt lighter and warm all over. I hugged him as he wiped my tears.

———•———

A few nights later, as Sam sat next to me on the couch in the living room, he smiled and looked into my eyes and spoke with a serious tone. "I need answers, Lyndie. I want to help you."

The time had come to share my story with him. I could do it. I realized I could trust this man with my pain. He wouldn't judge me. He really cared and wanted to help.

Sinking into the sofa, I took a deep breath and closed my eyes as my mind drifted back to that fateful life-altering day.

The streets of New York were crowded as Mom and I kept up with each other on the busy sidewalk. People moved in every which direction, eager to see the festive window displays and do their Christmas shopping. We strolled down Fifth Avenue and stopped at FAO Schwarz, the most famous toy store in the world. I couldn't help but be mesmerized by the displays and the giant teddy bear.

Mom and I had looked forward to this mother-daughter outing for months. I really couldn't think of a better way to celebrate my fourteenth birthday than to go to the Big Apple during Christmas vacation and check out the many things we didn't have at home. It was a tradition in Mom's family to take each of the girls here when they turned fourteen. My birthday was just a few weeks away, so here we were, dodging people on our way toward Thirty-Fourth Street.

"I'd like to take you to the legendary Macy's," said Mom.

"Mom, this is amazing! Dad said this store was huge, but this is immense."

"I'd like to find some more comfortable shoes."

"Ok. Can I please go over to the junior department?"

"Well … I guess it'd be all right. Meet me there in about fifteen minutes."

"Deal."

I ran over to a rack of cute hats. Maybe they'd have one to go with the green coat Dad bought me. Turning, I blinked in surprise as a cute boy, about seventeen or eighteen, was staring at me. My stomach flip-flopped. *Was I being watched?*

He shoved a hand through his wavy hair and walked toward me with an extra wide smile. He stopped so close, I could smell his cologne.

"Hi. My name is Anthony." He reached for my hand, his green eyes sparkling.

"I-I-I'm Lyndie." His touch sent tingles down my spine.

"You are bellissima."

"What?"

"That means beautiful in Italian."

My face grew hot, and I suddenly felt self-conscious.

His smile lingered. "You're not from around here, are you?"

"No." I tried to control the quiver in my voice, but it didn't work. "I'm … I'm visiting New York City with my mom. We live in Maryland."

"I'd love to see you again and show you around the city," he offered. "What are you doing later?"

"Oh, we're going to a Broadway show—Jersey Boys."

"Wow! I'm going there tonight too with my uncle. Maybe I'll see you."

"Okay." I noticed my mom coming toward us and decided it was time to wrap up the conversation. "Gotta go."

He nodded and turned away as Mom walked up with a frown on her face. "Who was the boy you were talking to?"

"Just a boy trying to be friendly."

"He was much older than you. Be careful! We're in New York City. Not everyone's intentions are good. You shouldn't talk to strangers."

"Oh, Mom." I resisted the impulse to roll my eyes. I was almost fourteen, after all. Hardly a baby.

The truth is, I couldn't stop thinking about Anthony the rest of the day. Mom was right about him being much older. But how flattering for an older boy to be interested in me.

I spent extra time fixing myself up for the play. I even talked Mom into letting me wear eye shadow with my mascara, hoping it would make me look older.

We arrived at the theatre with time to spare and went straight to our seats in front of the stage. I tried not to be too conspicuous as I looked around for Anthony. It wasn't long before I spotted him standing in the stalls towards the back of the auditorium. His smile broadened when our eyes met, and he nodded towards the back.

"Mom, I need to go to the restroom," I said.

I held my breath as she hesitated, then released it when she gave her permission. "All right, but hurry back, dear. The show is about to start soon."

My heart thumped all the way to the lobby.

Anthony strolled up and took my hand. "You look very pretty."

"Thank you," I said, blushing. I'd never had this attention from a boy, especially an older one.

"What are you doing after the play?" he asked.

I shrugged. "I don't know if my mom has plans."

"Well, there's a great Italian restaurant at the corner," he said. "They have the best pizza in town. My uncle and I are going there after the show. You like pizza, yeah?"

Who didn't like pizza? "Of course."

The lights flickered, and I hurried back to my seat. Throughout the show, all I could think of was Anthony and his adorable smile. He was so kind and polite. Definitely not someone to be afraid of. It felt nice to be with him.

The Jersey Boys finished their last song. "Mom, I'm hungry. I saw a pizzeria on the corner. Can we go?"

"Sure, sounds good, actually. New York pizza is supposed to be the best."

While we walked to the restaurant, I chewed my bottom lip and didn't make eye contact with Mom. I didn't want to accidentally say anything about meeting Anthony, I knew she wouldn't approve. Mom and Dad cautioned me about boys taking advantage.

Dad would take me on father/daughter dates and give me advice about boys. "If a boy is interested in you, he should respect you and treat you like a princess," he'd say. "The boy should want to come to your home and meet your parents." I felt myself pushing their advice aside. Anthony was extremely charming. I was excited to have a boy finally like me.

We sat in a booth near the front door, with me facing the restroom and Mom facing the entrance. I kept glancing over my shoulder to see if Anthony had come in.

A few minutes later, I noticed him standing around by the back of the restaurant, near the bathrooms. He motioned for me to come.

"Mom, I'm going to the restroom to wash my hands."

"Ok, I'll order when the waitress comes. Pepperoni, right?"

"Right. Please get me a Sprite."

Feeling guilty for lying, I walked back to the hallway where the restrooms were. A good-looking man winked at me. "Don't be long now, Anthony." Anthony grinned at me, and I melted. "So glad you came, Lyndie. Hey, my uncle and I drove here in my new sports car. I really want to show it to you. It's right out back."

A flutter of excitement—or was it fear—teased my stomach. "No, I couldn't. Mom thinks I'm washing my hands. I need to get back."

"No worries. The man you just passed by is my uncle Steve. He's very charming. He's gone to introduce himself to your mother and tell her he's the uncle of the boy you met today. Everything will be all right. He's even going to treat you all to pizza."

I relaxed just a bit. "Okay. I guess I can take a quick peek at your car."

"Great, let's go then."

Anthony took me by the hand and opened the backdoor. As soon as we stepped outside, everything seemed to happen in fast motion. Two men jumped out of a black sports utility vehicle. One put a cloth over my mouth, while the other grabbed me around the waist.

I turned towards Anthony, my eyes pleading for help. My

life flashed before my eyes. Every muscle in my body screamed. My heart hammered in my chest.

The man I believed to be Anthony's uncle appeared out of nowhere and helped shove me into the car. Dread crept up from the pit of my stomach and squeezed tight. I could no longer control my hands. Icy cold, I shook violently. *Why did I lie to my mom?* This is my fault. She tried to warn me. Paralyzed, I tried to scream, but terror seized my throat.

"Good job, Anthony," said one of the men. "Here's your money."

Anthony grinned, and my world went black.

———

When I regained consciousness, I found myself flat on a hard bench. My hands were bound; my mouth, gagged. *How in the world?* My head throbbed and my belly cramped with nausea. I felt trapped and confused. *Was I going to die?*

The small gray room they had deposited me in smelled like wet garbage and rancid food. It had nothing in it but an old couch and a tattered coffee table. Voices from the next room sounded angry and gruff.

"I'll give you twenty-five thousand for the girl," one man shouted.

"She's worth thirty thousand," the other man screamed.

"We agreed on twenty-five," said the woman.

"Okay. Twenty-five," said the second man, exasperated.

"Hand over the money and get out of here with the girl," shouted the first man.

Suddenly, my door flew open. A hefty, tattooed man lunged in and grabbed me.

"No!" I shouted. His nails dug into my flesh. Summoning all my strength, I kicked him. He cursed and slapped me across the side of my head. My body shook with fear and pain as he pulled me out the door.

Just when I didn't think it could get worse, he dragged me by my hair and threw me into the backseat of a car reeking of cigarettes and beer. What felt like hours later the car bounced along a gravel road and came to a halt. The man grabbed my arm, "Get out!"

He pushed me into an old, run-down house and shoved me into a dark dusty wood-paneled room. Terrified, cold, and hungry, I desperately needed to use the bathroom. The door creaked open. A woman, frowning heavily, entered. She ripped the gag off my mouth, and I grimaced.

"Please," I said, "I have to use the bathroom." She grabbed my arm, pulled me up, and pointed to a door in the corner of the room.

"I need my hands untied."

She stuck a gun in my ribs. "Okay, but don't you try nothin'."

The tiny gray-colored bathroom was not only filthy, but there was no toilet seat or toilet paper—only a dirty towel on the floor and cold water from the faucet. When I came out of the bathroom, she re-tied my hands behind my back. Pushing me onto the old, tattered mattress, she threw a scratchy wool blanket at me. "Here!"

"Please," I pleaded, "I want to go home. My father has money. He's a state senator. He'll pay anything to get me back."

"Shut up!" she said, slamming the door behind her.

Where am I? What are they going to do with me? Why was I so stupid to trust a stranger? Tears stung my eyes. *Why didn't I listen to my mother? Why did I trust that terrible boy? How could this nightmare be happening to me?* Questions kept shooting through my mind. Terrified and angry with myself for letting Anthony lure me into this horrible place, I started trembling and wailing uncontrollably.

Moments later, a tall, dark-haired man with large body-builder-shoulders came into the room. He slapped me so hard he knocked me off the mattress. "If you don't shut up, I got some more for you."

Terrified, I wrapped up in the scratchy blanket and cried myself to sleep.

The next morning, pain in my head pounded me awake from my half-asleep state. The door squeaked open, and I sat up. *Was that fried ham I smelled?* Sun seeped through the grimy window. The woman sauntered in with a smirk, dragging her hands through her bleached blonde hair and dark roots. She tossed a box of cornflakes and bottle of water on top of me. Untying my hands, she pointed toward the bathroom.

I tried to get my hands clean, but there was no soap. When I emerged from the bathroom, she held a gun in my face.

"Eat. Then we tell you the rules."

I gobbled down almost the entire box of cereal.

"Get the girl!" the man shouted.

The larger room contained a small TV with a VCR, a worn red couch, a torn brown, fake leather chair, and a small dining room table with four chairs. I looked helplessly at the man who had hit me as he sat at the table, smoking a cigarette.

"Sit down," he demanded. "I'm Hank, and this is Carol. We own you now. You'd better do what we say if you know what's good for you."

"But I want to go home," I sobbed. "My dad is rich. He works for the government. He'll pay whatever you want."

"Oh, we'll get his money, but we're keeping you. We've got big plans for you."

"You can't keep me here. My dad probably has the FBI looking for me."

"Shut your mouth!" His fist slammed into my mouth. "You'll get worse than that if you don't keep your trap shut and do as I say."

I tasted blood. I used my sleeve to dab it. I could feel my lips beginning to swell. Tears burst out like a broken dam, spilling down my face. My chin trembled like a small child, and I wished I could have been one, safely fastened to my mother's side.

Although Carol was the picture of hardness and misery, she still cringed when Hank struck me. It was then I knew she did what he told her to do, simply because she feared him.

Carol's skin was deeply wrinkled. Maybe from smoking. The lines made her appear old and weathered. She wore a revealing top, probably trying to expose what she thought was her best asset. Amidst her hard look, I noticed sadness in her eyes. Quite possibly from a life of abuse.

Hank did not look like the kind of man who would abduct children. He reminded me of a businessman who once came to our home trying to sell Daddy insurance. But this guy's eyes were vacant, and he had foul breath.

"We can't keep those clothes. Go change her out," ordered Hank.

Carol took me into the bathroom. "Get undressed." Embarrassed, I did as I was told, trying not to look at her gun. Considering her obedience to Hank, I knew she'd use it if he told her to.

She threw a towel at me and went out the bathroom door. Returning moments later, she had a change of clothes in her hands. They were too big, but at least they were clean. After I changed, she braided my hair and brought me back to Hank.

My skin crawled at the way his eyes scanned my body. "Well, she looks better now. She'll do." He looked me in the eyes. "What do they call you?"

"My name is Lyndie."

"From now on you'll be called Betty."

My cheeks burned. "But my name is Lyndie."

"And I said your name is Betty." He struck me. This time harder than before. I fell to the floor, trembling and sobbing. "Please take me home!"

23

"Stop bawling, or I'll smack you again!"

For the next couple of weeks, Hank and Carol attempted to be somewhat nice to me. Carol brought out a big box of Disney VCR tapes and let me watch them all day, guarding me the whole time. I was never allowed out of the house. They gave me all sorts of treats and foods a child might like—ice cream, candy, soda, hot dogs, mac and cheese, tacos, and even burgers and fries from McDonalds.

I enjoyed all the junk food. It was a change from the healthy snacks and nourishing meals at my home. Even as I relished the fast-food diet, I suspected they were treating me well according to their standards, since they wanted me to cooperate with them and get money from my dad.

After about two weeks, I got terrible stomachaches, and the movies became a bore. When I questioned them about school, Hank snickered, "We're going to give you an education."

Since I was locked inside and always watched, I couldn't even begin to think about escaping. I slept a lot and became depressed. I felt like I had a hole in my heart. I missed my family and wanted to be home with them.

One day, when Hank went to town and Carol was in the bathroom, I heard a noise outside. As I pulled the curtain aside in the front room, a man, standing on the porch, glared at me. He must have noticed my surprise as well. I jumped back quickly and shut the curtain, then ran back into my room and jumped into bed.

A few moments later, I heard a loud knock on the door. When no one answered, whoever it was knocked again even louder. Carol swore and mumbled to herself as she hurried out of the bathroom.

"May I help you?" she asked, cautiously.

"Hi. I'm Todd Jefferson, your neighbor from across the street. I'm a member of the school board in this county. I noticed you just moved in, and I wanted to acquaint you concerning our school and let you know where the bus stops. Just in case you have any children."

Carol hesitated for a moment. "No children here. Unfortunately, my husband and I can't have children."

"Well, I'm sorry, ma'am. I apologize for having bothered you. I'm just across the street if you ever need anything."

I knew the neighbor had seen me. Why didn't he say anything? The fear instilled in me by my captives didn't allow me to scream, though I desperately wanted to.

Carol slammed the door. I heard the roar of Hank's truck as it pulled into the yard. *Had Hank seen the neighbor leaving the house? Would Todd Jefferson talk to him?* It took Hank awhile before he came into the house, and I assumed the neighbor had said something to him. I smelled alcohol when Hank opened the front door and heard him raging on Carol.

"How could you be so stupid? What were you thinking, opening the door?"

I heard a loud smack and a crash. "We gotta get out of here tonight," Hank growled. "Fix me something to eat, then pack up. We're leaving as soon as it gets dark."

Carols eyes squinted and her teeth were clenched. The way she glared at me I knew she blamed me for the incident with the neighbor and for the beating Hank gave her. He had blackened both her eyes and left a deep gash on her cheek. This man was an evil monster.

Later in the night, she threw a peanut butter sandwich and a warm soda at me. I gobbled down the food and soda, then fell asleep.

I hadn't been asleep long when Carol's voice woke me. "Get up," she ordered. "We're leaving."

She tied my hands and put tape over my mouth, and Hank gruffly pushed me into the back of the truck. This environment was everything home was not. At home, I'd been loved and cared for, surrounded by happiness and peace.

I closed my eyes and envisioned Christmas night the year before my abduction. Driving in the car with my family to visit relatives, Dad had us play a game. "Let's see who can find the most lit-up Christmas trees." I couldn't stop laughing as Tommy tried singing "Jingle Bells." Oh, my family. What had I done? I couldn't handle this abuse.

I began to think of ways to end my life. To escape my thoughts, my mind drifted back to happier times. I thought of the day my little brother came into the world, all fresh and new, smelling like baby powder and breast milk. My mother beamed with delight in the hospital room. I snuggled into her with the baby and felt nothing but complete love. How desperately I missed them.

Tears. I'm all alone.

I was shaken out of my thoughts by the sound of Hank and Carol arguing. My head spun from his throat-constricting cigarette smoke.

"I told you to trade her for ransom money. She's nothing but trouble."

"Are you crazy, woman? I looked up her father, and he does work for the government."

"Hank, you're a fool. You know the FBI is involved in this. They'll mark the bills and have cops all over the place. We'll never get away with this."

"No, you're wrong. We'll make lots of money with her. You wait and see. I have big plans for this girl."

We traveled ten days. My arms were numb, my stomach growled, but I was afraid to cry for fear Hank would hit me. I wondered if the police were looking for me. My only relief was whenever Hank needed cigarettes or gas, and he'd stop at a store or gas station. Carol would untie me and rip the tape from my mouth.

"Get out," she ordered, gun to my ribs. "Use the bathroom and no funny business."

She stood outside the door until I finished. Then she sent me over to the car with Hank while she went to the bathroom. I hated it when Hank was the one who tied my hands. He always tied them tighter than she did.

When Carol got back into the car, she turned and put tape back on my mouth. This went on for another five days. I grew more and more thirsty and hungry, but they ignored me as usual. I was lucky if they gave me a cup of water, a handful of snacks, or even a piece of a sandwich. *What would I be doing now if I were home? Why didn't I listen to my mother and stay away from Anthony?*

Late one night, while off the main road, I felt myself being jostled around. The car soon stopped. Hank yanked me out.

"This house belonged to my grandfather who passed away," he told Carol. "Nobody's lived here for a long time. I made arrangements for the power to be turned back on."

Carol pushed me into a room, untied me, and ripped off the tape again. "Here." She handed me a water bottle.

I gulped it down and pleaded for something to eat before she turned to leave the room. "Please?"

Without answering, she stepped out. When she returned, she threw me a half-eaten bag of chips, a loaf of bread, and a jar of peanut butter.

I shoved a handful of chips in my mouth.

"Hurry and eat," she ordered. "You have cleaning to do."

For the next couple hours, I scrubbed bathrooms and floors, vacuumed carpets, and washed clothes. Exhausted, I sat down on the green itchy couch to fold laundry. Fearing what they might do to me, I tried hard not to fall asleep, but sleep won in the end.

⌒4⌒

No Longer Free

I awakened to Hank's pungent beer breath in my face. "Wake up, little princess. It's time for your debut." He tossed me a giant Hershey bar, which I immediately gobbled.

Carol handed me a bag containing shampoo, soap, and a towel. "Go clean yourself up but don't get your hair wet." The nightgown she laid out on the bed was much too grown up for me, but at least it was clean. The underwear looked like it came from Victoria's Secret.

"Come here," she ordered. "I'm going to color and blow-dry your hair." She quickly and sloppily slathered goo all over my head, burning my skin, and almost dripping the bleach-smelling dye into my eyes and mouth. A few minutes later, my brunette locks had become a streaky blonde mess. Finally, she smeared dark red lipstick and rouge on me. I glanced in the mirror and felt estranged to myself. Hatred for Carol and Hank poured over me. They had stolen my childhood, and it was about to be stolen even more.

"She's ready," she hollered to Hank.

He entered the room. "Why, there now! You look so pur-tee." He laughed, took me by the hand, and led me into a room in the back of the house. They had a camera set up with a raggedy black cloth as a backdrop. The small bed had a frilly pink bedspread with a large brown stuffed teddy bear on top.

"Go lie on the bed," he ordered.

Everything in me wanted to run. When I hesitated, he took out his gun and made me get into several nasty positions. First, he took photos of me with my clothes on. When he told me to take them off, I refused. He punched me in the stomach; but still, I disobeyed his orders. When I wouldn't budge, he punched me so hard in the face my nose began to bleed, and my eye swelled up.

"Why you little— Carol! Get in here!"

Carol ran into the room, stopped short, and gasped. But she knew better than to question Hank. The same thing might happen to her.

"It's going to be a while before I can take more pictures of her," Hank complained, "I want you to tie her up. She gets nothing to eat until she learns to obey." Jerking me by my hair, he glared into my eyes. "You better do what I say if you don't want anything to happen to your little brother."

Oh, no! This monster better not hurt my little brother, Tommy! I was horrified but didn't dare say a word.

Banished to my bedroom, my face hurt too much to cry. I lay in the dark, moaning and shaking. This has to be what hell is like—imprisonment and torture. I ached for the love and comfort of my home, wishing I could die.

I was tied up for hours on end and practically starved to death as days slipped into a week. Whenever I begged Carol to let me use the bathroom, she untied me. I was allowed one glass of warm water twice a day. Feeling sick, I once again contemplated taking my life. I searched the room for something to hang myself, but it wouldn't be that easy.

Once the bruises healed, the hideous photo sessions resumed. I closed my eyes, remembering what my grandmother used to tell me when I was afraid. "God has a good plan and purpose for your life. He loves you so much. He gave you a big, strong guardian angel who watches over you all the time." I imagined this majestic angel with a flaming sword, and for a few brief moments, I wasn't afraid.

One day, Hank burst through the front door after a trip to town. "We gotta get out of here," he yelled. "There's cops snooping all over this town, looking for the girl."

I was thankful we were leaving again, realizing there wouldn't be any more photo shoots for a while. This time I wasn't gagged or tied up.

"I want no marks on her body," I heard Hank tell Carol. But I was far from safe and comfortable. The whole trip to wherever, Carol sat in the backseat with a gun aimed at me.

I had too much time alone with my thoughts. I couldn't handle the beatings anymore. And the abuse and humiliation were worse. Hank's grabbing me during the sessions. I resolved, next time, I'd let Hank shoot me instead.

We drove across many miles of farmland, but at least they fed me fairly regularly. I wondered why until Hank remarked, "You're getting too skinny. We need to fatten you up."

We drove for almost a week. Hank would occasionally pull off the road for a few hours to get some sleep. I guessed they were afraid to stop at a motel since my picture was probably all over the news. I wondered if the neighbor from the school board ever realized I was the missing girl. Maybe he called the police.

As the sun set one night, Hank pulled into a gas station. Carol grabbed a hooded sweatshirt and roughly jerked it over my head. Nobody was around except the attendant.

Carol and I sat in the car for an extremely long time, waiting on Hank. I was miserably hot in the sweatshirt, but I knew I didn't dare attempt to remove it.

"Where were you?" Carol growled at Hank.

"I finally got my partner on the phone. He said the old farmhouse he was telling me about is only three hours away. We can hide out there as long as we need to." Hank tossed me a sandwich, chips, and a soda. Thinking we might end up in the new area for a long time, I tried to memorize the landmarks and signs.

About a half-hour later, we came to a small town with a Motel 6, a drugstore, a barbershop, an elementary school, a Piggly-Wiggly, and a restaurant called Rosie's Place. Since there was no police station, Hank took a chance and parked behind the restaurant.

"Get down on the floor."

He returned with three Styrofoam meal containers and three Styrofoam cups. Getting back behind the wheel, he went a little farther, and he pulled into an abandoned park.

"Get out," he ordered. "We're eating here."

Opening my container, I devoured the bacon, scrambled eggs, and pancakes like it couldn't get down fast enough.

A few hours later, we turned off the road to Highway 75 and onto a dirt road. Plainview Lane led us to another dirt road. I squinted to read the sign— something like Dobbs. We approached a large iron gate connected to a rusty fence surrounding a farmhouse. In the dim light of the headlights, I thought I could make out woods in the distance.

We stepped into a house that didn't look like it'd been lived in for years. Talk about old and dusty. Surprisingly, the appliances worked, but the fridge wasn't very cold.

Hank knew how to get to me. He told me he had a friend who lived close to where my little brother went to school. He warned me if I gave them any trouble, his friend would hurt my brother.

Hank didn't waste time before taking pictures of me again. I went from feeling disgraced and humiliated to just plain numb. The picture-taking went on for almost a year until the day Hank said to Carol, "We're getting low on money. We need to send her out soon."

Send her out? Although I didn't exactly know what they meant, knowing Hank and Carol, it couldn't be good.

Hank's old partner, Joe, showed up. He reminded me of a weasel with greasy, slicked back black hair and rotten teeth. As much as I hated and feared Carol and Hank, Joe terrified me even more. He had a filthy mouth—barely able to form a sentence without cursing. He looked at me the way a lion salivates

31

over a steak. And when no one was looking, he grabbed at my body.

Joe and Hank stayed up late drinking, smoking, and talking. The next morning, they left and during the following weeks of Hank's absence, Carol gave me the nicest gift. She let me go outside. Although I felt like a prisoner with a tall hemmed-in-fence all around me, I hadn't been outside by myself since I was abducted, and it felt wonderful. I ran all over the backyard, and I delighted in watching butterflies land on flowers. At one point, a chipmunk almost crawled up on my lap. I ran into the house and got him some stale bread with peanut butter. Although nervous of me at first, he ate right from my hand. Chip. That's what I'd call him. I'd made a new friend.

I began to bring Chip food each day, and he'd sit near me, munching away. I told him what I was going through and imagined he listened and understood. *I hope Hank never returns*, I thought.

One night, I was awakened to the sound of yelling. Oh no. Hank! Wait. W*as a child crying?* I held my breath to listen more intently.

"Another mouth to feed. Are you out of your mind?" said Carol. "You want more cops after us?"

"Shut up," shouted Hank. "I know what I'm doing. Betty's ready to go out now, and we can start priming this little one for photos."

Hank banged my door open and flipped on the light. Standing next to him was a fragile little girl with red hair and freckles, sobbing and shaking.

"This is Susan. You need to tell her what she has to do to get by here." He glared at me, shoved her into the room, and slammed the door.

"I want my mommy and daddy," Susan sobbed uncontrollably. "I wanna go home."

I put my arm around her and told her to sit down. And when

she was ready, we talked. Ten years old. That's all she was. I knew only too well the fear she was experiencing, and I ached for her.

"You have to stop crying," I urged her. "If you don't, Hank will hurt you. I promise I'll help you get home." *What had I just told her? How could I help her escape when I couldn't even help myself?* But suddenly I felt myself charged with more fiery determination than ever. Yes, I would help little Susan escape. I had to.

Hank disappeared for another few days, giving Susan and I the opportunity to explore outside. I introduced her to Chip, and he licked her hand, bringing a smile to her eyes.

When Hank returned, he ordered, "Get her ready." Carol came to me with clothes, shoes, and make-up, then made me try on everything. I could hardly walk in the high heels, and the clothes made me look like a streetwalker. My sneakers and sweats never sounded so good.

Carol painted me with heavy make-up, clothed me in a revealing outfit, spraying so much perfume on me that I sneezed.

"Time for a car ride," Hank smirked. Terror gripped me. "Here, drink this." He handed me a glass of something from a bottle. When I turned my head, he twisted my arm and grabbed my throat until I had swallowed the concoction. I coughed and gagged as it burned its way down.

"It'll make you relax," he said.

My head spun as we turned into the parking lot of a Motel 6. "Come on!" ordered Hank, pulling me out.

A heavy-set, slack-jawed man, wearing jeans and an undershirt opened door 215. I stumbled as Hank pushed me toward the man. Apparently satisfied, after looking me over from head to toe, the man handed Hank a wad of cash.

Hank stuffed it into his pocket. "I'll be waiting outside in my car," he told me.

The foul smelling man gripped my arm. "You're staying here with me. We're going to have some fun."

Hank sneered. "Be nice to the gentleman."

Once the door closed, the man threw me down on the bed. The room spun. When his heavy body fell on top of me, it knocked the wind out of me. I must have passed out. When I snapped out of it, my clothes were off, and I hurt in places I'd never hurt before.

Grabbing my clothes, I ran into the bathroom and threw up. My head pounded from whatever Hank had forced down my throat. I tried to scrub off the man's stench, along with my smeared makeup, until my skin appeared bright red.

Finally, Hank called my name, and I quickly but cautiously emerged from the bathroom.

Hank laughed. "Did you have fun in there, Betty?"

I wanted to throw up again, but I put my head down and wouldn't look at either of them.

Back in the car, Hank patted my head. "You're going to do fine, my little moneymaker."

I need to protect Susan from this, I thought. *I need to get her out here before this happens to her.* The feeling became so desperate, it lit a fire in me. Whatever it would take, I had to find a way to get out from under Carol and Hank's watchful eyes.

Hank could tell I cared for the girl. He began to threaten to use Susan if I didn't do as he told me to. For the next five years, Hank dropped me off to spend time with the same disgusting man or another just like him three to four times a week.

One night, I noticed he put a couple of pills in the drink. I tried spitting them out, but Hank held my mouth closed until he was sure I'd swallowed everything. Something didn't feel right. As we walked to the hotel room, I felt lighthearted and giddy. This time there wasn't just one man waiting, but a whole group of them. Sickness enveloped me, and I ran to the bathroom. When Hank picked me up, the men complained they didn't get what they had paid for, but he wouldn't return their money.

Susan quickly became the little sister I never had, and I soon nicknamed her Suzi. Hank and Carol had left her alone, at least for the time being. They let her play with things Carol bought her, or they'd allow her to watch videos. Sometimes I even saw Carol treat her nicely. I figured maybe she identified Suzi as the child she'd never have. I also decided I was making them enough money they didn't need to use Suzi—yet. When I overheard Hank tell Carol it was time to take pictures of Suzi, I knew I had to do something. I couldn't let them ruin her the way they ruined me. Right then I promised Suzi I'd get her out of there.

The next afternoon Hank went out to find more clients for me. When he returned within an hour, I saw horror in his eyes. "The town is crawling with cops asking questions," he whispered to Carol. "We have to get out of here now. We'll use the old van in the barn. I bought parts to fix it while I was in town. I'm not going to chance it with the car." He went out and worked on the van, while Carol hurriedly gathered our stuff.

When dark descended, Hank brought the van around, and we jumped in. Carol bound Suzi's hands and put tape over her mouth. I begged them not to, but they said they didn't trust her not to scream. They left me alone, though, probably figuring I knew the consequences well enough not to cross them.

I held on to Suzi and kept repeating, "I'm here." Avoiding the town, Hank traveled through the woods behind the house. Next, we drove the narrow roads through the fields beyond the woods. It was a long time before we got back on a main road. When we did, we drove for several days, stopping only when Hank had to put gas in the van. He even brought gas cans with us so we wouldn't have to stop as often. We went in the bushes when we needed a bathroom.

Early one morning, I spotted a roadside sign that announced: Welcome to Utah. I was stunned at how far we'd come.

Hank turned to Carol, "I have a cousin in Provo who just got out of jail. He said we could stay with him." I suddenly realized Hank's whole family was probably corrupt.

We pulled up to a gas station convenience store while Suzi slept soundly beside me. I had to go so bad I thought I'd burst. "I really have to go," I pleaded.

"Take her and get us some food. And don't forget my cigarettes," Hank ordered. When we exited the car, I turned around quickly and memorized the car's license plate. Carol let me into the restroom. "I'm going to get supplies while Hank pumps gas. He's right out front, so don't try anything stupid."

Locking the door behind me, I immediately spotted an open window. I peeked outside and spotted a flatbed farm truck just under the window, parked right up next to the wall. My heart raced with excitement. This is it. My chance to escape! I can get help for Suzi. Without hesitation I shoved hard with all my might to open the window a bit more. I pushed myself through and fell onto the truck's flatbed. I prayed the driver would get me out of there before I was discovered.

———•———

"Well, Sam, you know the rest," I said. "You and your truck really did rescue me. I just wish I could have seen the look on Carol and Hank's faces when they realized I'd gotten away. I only pray they didn't take it out on Suzi."

Sam's eyes glistened with tears, but he closed them and immediately began to pray. "Lord, heal Lyndie from all this, and please protect Suzi." When he finished, his eyes shown with deep compassion. "What you did took real courage. Was the phone call you made when you first got here to the police about Suzi?"

I nodded. "Yes. But I dialed star-sixty-nine so they wouldn't track your number. I gave them the make, model, and license plate of Hank's van. I remembered the gas station had a sign that read Bob's Gas. I gave them Suzi's, Carol's, and Hank's names and descriptions. The police promised to contact the FBI to assure Suzi would be rescued."

"Well, I think I have good news for you," Sam said. "A few

days after you arrived here, I went into town to get food and a haircut. While sitting in the barber chair, I heard on the news a couple had been apprehended along with a young girl they'd kidnapped. The news went on to say the girl had been reunited with her parents. The newscaster reported when the family was interviewed, the little girl made a statement something like, 'I'll never forget what you've done, sister, thanks for keeping your promise.'"

For the first time in years, I cried tears of joy.

≈5≈

Fear Takes Control

In the evening, Sam searched the internet and found Carol and Hank were each expected to be sentenced to twenty-five years. When he showed it to me, I broke down, "Thank You, God! They can't hurt anyone ever again." Sam held me while I cried, but my tears were joyful knowing Suzi had been set free. Never would she have to do the horrific things I was forced to do. She still had her childhood. Although mine was stolen, I was grateful I could help someone else. I smiled as a thought popped into my head. Maybe when Suzi and I are older and have families of our own, we can be reunited.

Then Sam brought me back to reality. "You need to go home, Lyndie."

Home. The word frightened me. *How could I ever go home after what I'd experienced with all those horrible, disgusting men? What if my parents found out what I'd done?*

Sam seemed to be reading my thoughts. "Lyndie, you're not responsible for the heinous things those men did to you. God loves you, and He's already forgiven you. He wants to heal you from your past. He has a bright future for you."

His words brought comfort and peace to my heart, reminding me again of the similar words my grandmother had spoken to me years earlier. I stayed silent for a moment, allowing them to sink in.

Still holding me, Sam asked, "Do you want to call your parents?"

I shook my head. "Not now, Sam."

"Ok. I know this is difficult for you." He patted my back.

"I'd be willing to talk to them first if you'd like. I have a little money tucked away, and I'd be pleased to use it to help you get home."

"Oh, Sam, you'd do that for me?" I pulled away from him. The sincerity and acceptance I saw in his wrinkled face threatened my tears to start again. I took a deep breath and blinked them away. "Thank you for everything, Sam."

The next day was my nineteenth birthday. Knowing I hadn't had a birthday celebration in several years, Sam took me to the county fair to celebrate.

We had a blast. I ate cotton candy, candied apples, and hot dogs. We played concession games, and Sam won a pink teddy bear for me. "Her name is Sarah," I informed Sam.

We rode every ride at least once. My favorite part was the animal exhibits, including horses, cows, pigs, ducks, chickens, and a donkey. We even watched a cow give birth. I made up my mind right then I'd like to be a veterinarian someday. When we met a man at the exhibit who had a pet ferret, I thought of Chip, the chipmunk who'd been my friend and confidant. I said a silent prayer, "Please, God, keep Chip safe."

I fell asleep in the truck on the way home. Once again, Sam carried me into the house in his warm, strong arms, and I thought, *Jesus' arms must be like Sam's.*

I slept late the next morning. A wonderful aroma from the kitchen eventually lured me out of bed. Sam had made pancakes with fresh blueberries from his garden. On the counter was a surprise birthday cake with my name on it.

I stopped to admire it. "Did you make this cake, Sam?"

"I sure did. It was one of my Sarah's recipes. Carrot cake was her favorite."

"It's mine too. How did you know?"

"I guess a little birdie told me," he kidded.

He cleared his throat before continuing. "I've been checking on flights for you, and I figure you can be on your way soon.

I'll call your parents to let them know you're coming since you're nervous about that."

"You're going to fly me home? I expected you'd put me on a bus or a train."

He shook his head as he flipped a pancake. "Not a chance. You've all waited too long for this. When I phone your parents, I'm sure they'll be more than eager to meet you at the airport." Sam's idea sounded good to me. It gave me more time to prepare for what I'd say when I finally reunited with my family. I'd missed and longed for them for so many years. Yet now, after all this time, I had mixed feelings of excitement and apprehension.

"All right, Sam," I assured him. "So, when do I leave?"

"I can get you a flight next Friday morning. There's one stop in Chicago, and then you'll arrive in Maryland later in the evening."

Nine days. Only nine days! How I'd miss Sandy, the rides on Daisy, and most of all, Sam. He was the grandpa I never knew.

"Don't think of it as good-bye," Sam said. "Why, you and your family can come visit me anytime."

He was right of course, and I began to plan and daydream about my upcoming reunion with my family.

Each day before I left, Sam and I took long rides on Daisy and Rocket. Sandy trailed right beside us. Sam told me how much Jesus loved me and talked to me about heaven and how wonderful it was going to be when we all were there.

And then it was time to leave. I got up extra early that morning and went out to the barn to say my farewells. Sandy stayed by my side the entire time.

"I love you, Daisy, and will miss you so much." She licked my face with her big tongue, seeming to understand I was leaving.

"We need to eat and get moving, Missy," Sam called, tears teasing his eyes. "I want to get you there on time." When I sat down in front of my breakfast, he handed me an envelope. I pulled out three photos: one of Sandy and me, one of Daisy, and one of Sam and Sarah. I wiped a tear away as he handed me two other presents. When I opened the first, I gasped at the beauty of the Bible with my name engraved in gold. Inside the second package was a small purse and wallet, and inside the wallet was a picture of Sam and me we'd taken at the fair. The wallet also contained a wad of hundred-dollar bills.

I looked from the money to Sam and shook my head. "I can't take this."

"Yes, you can. I don't want you traveling without any money. You can use it to get yourself a puppy when you get home. You can even name it Sam if you'd like." He laughed, sending warmth way down into my heart.

Home! I thought of the dog my family had when I was kidnapped. Lady, a cocker spaniel, looked like the one in the movie *Lady and the Tramp*. She was eight years old when I was taken. She couldn't possibly still be alive.

I smiled at the thought of a puppy. I gave Sandy a big hug and kiss and in return, she gave me her paw.

"I'm going to miss you, girl," I managed to choke out. "Take care of Sam."

At the airport, Sam took my hand and prayed for a safe flight and a glorious reunion with my parents. He grabbed my suitcase out of the truck and walked me to the security gate, tears glistening in his eyes.

"Remember, Lyndie, God loves you. He's always right there whenever you need him."

I gave Sam the biggest hug I could and then walked through the security check, not allowing myself to look back. With time to kill before the plane left, I settled in to read a magazine.

Waiting for my flight should have been exciting, but it felt as if every single man in the airport was looking at me. One bald, heavyset man winked at me. To avoid any man's gaze, I kept my eyes cast down. It was as if I were wearing a sign "Sex for Hire."

Relieved when they finally called my group, I boarded the plane and hoped a woman would be seated next to me. Instead, a harmless looking middle-aged man in a business suit sat down beside me, barely giving me any notice as he took out his laptop. A gold band encircled his ring finger. *He must be married with at least two kids*, I told myself.

Immediately the scenes of the men who raped me, who also wore wedding bands, bore into my mind. I was so preoccupied with fighting the memories. I didn't realize his hand had dropped to the inside of my thigh. Slowly stroking my thigh, he leaned over and whispered, "Hey, gorgeous, we could have a lot of fun together tonight."

My body began to shake. Startled, he jerked his hand away and jumped into the aisle. I snatched my bag from under the seat and ran toward the restroom. Locking the door behind me, I started to hyperventilate. *Oh no, it's happening again. Will men always think I'm the kind of woman who likes to attract them and have sex with them?*

After some time, the flight attendant rapped on the door to check on me. I patted cold water on my face and decided I'd look for another seat. Opening the door, I bumped into another man who looked to be in his late twenties. Thankfully, he made no comment, and I stepped past him. I spotted an empty seat next to a middle-aged woman with graying hair and took it, with relief washing over me.

I closed my eyes and turned my thoughts to my family. *How can I tell them what I'd been through?* I agonized. They're my parents. It was easier with Sam. He was a stranger—well, he started out that way. And he never judged me. I imagined how devastating it would be for my mother to know her little girl had done such terrible things with all those men.

I opened my eyes and noticed the man sitting across the

aisle was staring at me. When he caught my eye, he winked—and I shuddered. I'd seen that look in men's eyes before. It disgusted me then and did even more so now. *Can't I go anywhere without being leered at? Will men always be able to look at me and tell the dirty things I've done?*

By the time the plane landed, I felt as though I were suffocating. Nearly running from the gate, I tried to stay clear of the man who winked at me. I went to Dunkin' Donuts and ordered a coffee and a donut. It was two hours and thirty minutes until my next flight. The longer I sat, the more nervous I became as a movie of all the things Hank forced me to do whirled through my mind. My body shook violently, and I ran to the restroom and threw up. Splashing cold water on my face, I took a moment to regain my composure and was able to get back to Dunkin' Donuts for ginger ale to settle my stomach.

The people at the table next to me were talking excitingly about their vacation. "It was paradise," the woman said, fingering a colorful lei. "It felt as though all my problems were fading as I walked along the beautiful beaches and witnessed the breathtaking sunsets. What an escape!"

Hawaii! I'd always wanted to visit their beautiful islands. My dad had promised us we'd take a family vacation there one day.

Such a long time ago, I sighed. Standing up to board my plane, I was once again overcome by fear. *I can't do this.* It'll kill my parents to know what I've done. As I passed a ticket counter for Hawaiian Airlines, I veered from my path and instead approached the ticket agent.

I took a deep breath. "How much is a one-way ticket to Hawaii?"

The attractive young female ticket attendant smiled. "We have a special going on for flights to Honolulu. You can even get a better price if you fly standby. We have two more flights yet today."

Before I could talk myself out of it, I bought a ticket. The first flight would leave in fifty-five minutes. The agent said I'd have a better chance on the later one, but I thought I'd give the first one a try.

A half-hour later I was boarding the plane. Hawaiian music filled the air, and the flight attendants were dressed in aloha attire.

Settled in my seat, I realized by now Sam must have contacted my parents. My heart dropped — I'd let Sam and my parents down. I'll call Sam when I land in Honolulu, I promised myself.

My wayward thoughts were interrupted, however, as a young, good-looking man sat down next to me.

6

Finding Peter

"Are you all right?" He smiled, and I swear his teeth were so white they glistened.

Before I could answer, he continued, "You look lost. My name's Peter Stanton." He extended his hand, his smile widening as our eyes met. His eyes were kind and deep, as blue as the ocean. Instantly I decided he was the most handsome man I'd ever seen. I couldn't help but think he looked as if he belonged on the cover of *Gentlemen's Quarterly*.

"Is this your first trip to the islands?" he inquired.

I swallowed and squeaked out, "Yes."

"Do you have family there?"

I shook my head. "No." I swallowed again. "This is my ... birthday gift," I lied.

His face lit up. "Well, Hawaii is my home, and there's nowhere nicer to celebrate a birthday. I'd love to show you around." He smiled again, and I knew I'd accept his offer.

"Thanks ... Peter."

"Here's my number." He handed me a business card embossed in gold.

Peter Stanton

Entertainment & Promotions

808-555-9965

I took the card as he asked, "And what's your name? It would be helpful to know that if we're going to sightsee together."

Taking a deep breath, I lied again. "Lyndie Butler." At least I'd given him the correct first name. It was nice not to have to go by Betty anymore.

We chatted throughout the entire flight, discussing the many things to do and see on Oahu. My excitement grew as Peter described the islands. He was smart, gorgeous, and quite the gentleman. He not only treated me with kindness and respect, but he was interested in me as a person. Before we landed in Honolulu, I fell head over heels in love with Peter Stanton.

When we departed the plane, he squeezed my hand gently, "Call soon, Lyndie." As he stepped away to retrieve his luggage, I went to hail a cab, since I only had a carry-on.

When a taxi stopped the driver asked, "Where to?"

I loved his Hawaiian accent. "Do you know of a hotel with reasonable rates?'

"Sure do."

He took me to a cute little motel a few blocks from the beach. "Good weekly rates here," he said.

I thanked and paid him, then went inside. The motel was $125 per week, well within my budget. I'd call Sam before the week was up, I decided. Until then I'll rest here in the islands until I gather the courage to face my family.

⤳7⤳

My Journey in Paradise

The next morning, I was stunned by the beauty I witnessed before me. Wow! I'm really in Hawaii. I can't believe it.

As I stood on the balcony of my motel room, it started to drizzle. I looked up at the mountains and beheld the most magnificent rainbow I'd ever seen. God's promise. The words echoed in my mind as I thought of my parents and what they must be feeling. I pushed the thoughts away. Tomorrow I'll phone Sam and tell him where I am, and I'll make arrangements to go home to Maryland. But first I need some time to myself.

I walked a couple blocks and entered a small restaurant. I was surprised when the scrambled eggs came with rice. Hawaiian music kept me company as I ate and filled my heart with peace. Out on Kalakaua Avenue, all the clothes in the boutique shops were so colorful I couldn't resist. I entered a quaint shop and purchased a bathing suit, matching beach dress, sunscreen, and sandals with flowers on them. The friendly salesgirl explained to me the flowers printed on the dress were called plumerias and leis were often made with them. From then on, I was delighted by the many stands selling plumeria in white, yellow, and pink.

I returned to my motel room, put on my new bathing suit, grabbed a towel, and walked to the beach. The ocean was greenish-blue and clear as glass. I was amazed to discover I could look down through the water and see my feet.

As I spread my towel and sat down to enjoy the beautiful scenery, I couldn't help but notice how happy everyone seemed. *Why wouldn't they be? They're in paradise.*

Jumping up, I glanced at my legs. Oh no, they were a bright shade of pink. I must have dozed off. Enough sun for today. Grabbing my things, I hurried back to the motel. Digging in my purse, I found Peter's business card. Not wanting to phone him too late, I took a quick shower. When I dialed his number, he answered on the first ring.

"I was afraid you might not call, and I'd never see you again," he said. "I'm so glad you did. Would you like to have dinner with me?"

"Love to," I responded eagerly, my heart already racing at the sound of his voice.

"Pick you up at seven. Where are you staying?"

"At the Pulani on Kekua Street."

As soon as I hung up, I borrowed an iron from the front desk and pressed an adorable, pink dress Sam had bought me as part of my going-home wardrobe.

Peter was right on time. He was beyond handsome in his white pants and teal Hawaiian print shirt, and he smelled fabulous. He took me to a wonderful restaurant known for its lobster. We sipped on white wine and looked out at the ocean. We laughed often throughout the evening. He told me all about growing up on Oahu in a military family. He learned to surf at a young age and loved it.

"Would you like to take a walk on the beach?" Peter asked.

"Sure, I'd love to." A smile turned up the corners of his lips. We took off our shoes and walked quietly together, enamored by the thousands of stars and the brilliance of the moon glistening on the ocean. What a romantic night!

"This is beautiful," I said, my heart so full I thought it might burst.

"It sure is," Peter responded, as he slipped his arm around my waist. "So are you." He drew me close, and his lips barely brushed mine.

"You are absolutely lovely, Lyndie. I love your smile."

A simple thank you was all I could manage to say.

He gently ran his fingers through my hair, then drew me close again. I melted at his embrace. This time his tender kiss lasted a little longer. For the first time it seemed all right to let a man get close to me. He wasn't at all rough like the men I'd been with. And then he released me.

"I'm sorry. I shouldn't have done that. You hardly know me. I guess it just feels so right with you."

"It's okay. I know what you mean. It feels right with you too."

We walked hand-in-hand back to Peter's red Porsche. Leaning my head back as he drove, the wind blowing my long hair intoxicated me. He reached over and squeezed my hand just before we arrived at my motel.

He walked me to my room and kissed me on the forehead. "Want to go sightseeing around the island tomorrow?"

"Sounds like fun. I'd love to."

"Pick you up at eight. We'll have breakfast first. And don't forget your bathing suit."

When I finally fell asleep, I dreamt of Peter, and being wrapped in his arms as he kissed me.

———•———

I got up early to make sure I'd look perfect for Peter. I spent extra time on my hair and make-up. Peter showed up with a special surprise, a beautiful lei of pink plumerias. Another excuse for him to kiss me?

"Pretty flowers for a pretty lady," he said, as he kissed me again, this time ever so gently on the cheek.

Peter took me to an adorable outdoor cafe for breakfast. As we ate, he reached over and took my hand. "I'm so glad I was on your flight."

"Me too," I smiled shyly.

We spent the day crisscrossing the island of Oahu. We drove

up the Pali Highway to the Pali lookout, and I marveled at the majestic green mountains. We went swimming at a beach called Chinamen's Hat, deriving its name from the shape of a little island by the beach. Then we drove to Kahuku and swam with the huge turtles.

Our next stop was Haliewa, a quaint little surfing community on the North Shore. Peter reminisced during lunch how his father had taken him to the North Shore as a young boy to teach him how to surf. Later, on a walk around the village, Peter spotted a frilly white dress hanging in a boutique window.

"Go try it on, Lyndie."

I was happy to oblige, and when I came out of the dressing room, both Peter and the salesgirl gasped.

"Wow," the girl exclaimed, "this dress was made for you! I've seen other girls try it on, but no one looks as perfect in it as you." She reached over and took flowered barrettes from under the counter. "Put these in your hair," she suggested. "They match the embroidery on the dress."

"She's right," Peter commented. "They look awesome and match perfectly with the dress." He turned to the salesgirl. "We'll take them and also the sandals over there."

Before I could protest Peter said, "The young lady will wear these to go."

He slipped his arm around me. "Let's go have a romantic dinner."

"Ok. Sounds great. But now since I'm dressed up as your queen, let's go to Ala Moana and let me pick out a nice outfit for you too." I chose a turquoise silk shirt, white pants, and beige Docker loafers.

"You have good taste, Lyndie."

I smiled and gazed up at him. "I sure do."

Peter took me to an exclusive restaurant in Hawaii Kai. I was pleased to see it had a band and a dance floor.

We sat down, and Peter ordered a Caesar salad, which the

waiter made right at our table. For appetizers we had a lobster bruschetta and steamed asparagus.

Peter said, "Have you ever eaten Mahi Mahi?"

"No, what is it?

"It's one of the most popular fish of the islands. Trust me. You'll love it."

Peter ordered a bottle of wine to go with dinner. The wine warmed my insides, but not as warm as I felt when Peter held me close on the dance floor.

After our dance Peter excused himself. A few minutes after he returned, the singer announced, "The next song is dedicated to the pretty lady down there." He pointed at me and began to sing, "The Way You Look Tonight." Peter smiled and led me back out to the dance floor. I wrapped my arms around Peter's neck and inhaled his scent, earth mixed with musk. He sang along with the music as he looked deeply into my eyes.

Later, we drove back to my hotel, the top down on Peter's red Porsche. The stars twinkling above sprinkled a dreamy light all around us. What a perfect evening with a cool breeze blowing through my hair, Peter holding my hand, and my head on his shoulder.

"This is a magical night," he whispered.

"Umm, yes, it is."

This time when Peter said good night, his kiss lingered a little longer. "Spend the day with me again tomorrow?"

"Of course," I whispered.

My dreams that night were filled with beautiful cascading waterfalls and Peter proposing to me.

"Put on a bathing suit." Peter's eyes danced with excitement. "We're going to the Pipeline Masters on the North Shore. You're going to love this." Then he paused, and the light in his eyes dimmed slightly. "Sorry, but I won't be able to take you to dinner tonight. I have to go to my business establishment and make sure everything is running like it should."

I nodded and forced a smile. "That's all right," I said, trying to mask my disappointment. Once again, I found myself wondering what he actually did for a living. All he had shared with me was he owned some exclusive clubs. *Well, it doesn't matter,* I told myself. *I have the whole day with him.*

On our way to the North Shore, Peter stopped at a local restaurant. A Hawaiian lady, who seemed to be the owner, gave Peter a tight hug. "So happy, Mr. Peter. I see you got you a pretty wahine."

Peter laughed and put his arm around me, then he lifted my hand to his lips and kissed it. I squeezed his hand in return.

A waitress approached us and giggled. "Keep this one," she said with a wink. "She looks like a sweet lady."

"I'm planning to," Peter answered, his voice suddenly husky with emotion," for as long as she'll have me."

My heart skipped a beat, as joy swept over me. I'd fallen in love with Peter "at first sight," as the saying goes, and I was certain he loved me too, though he hadn't actually said the words.

After a wonderful meal we drove around the island, the colors of the ocean and the mountains nearly taking my breath away. "I could live here forever," I said.

Peter took my hand. "I hope so."

The North Shore was hosting a surfing competition called the "Pipeline Masters." We found the perfect spot on Pipeline beach to watch the contest. I was awestruck at the skill of the surfers as they maneuvered their boards on the waves, making it look so easy.

The sun sparkled on the ocean, and a slight breeze kept us comfortable throughout the afternoon. Peter sat close to me on the blanket as we shared food and drinks we'd bought on the way. "Another perfect day." His eyes searched mine.

My heart fluttered. "Yes, it is."

"You make it perfect, Lyndie." His words caressed me as he smiled and brushed my cheek with a kiss.

Peter was silent on the drive back, and I wondered if I'd said or done something wrong. At last, he spoke. "I don't think I'm going to be able to do this."

I frowned. "Do what?"

He glanced at me long enough to say, "Stay away from you tonight."

I swallowed, relieved to know we were both still on the same track. "I know what you mean. I'm going to miss you too."

"Maybe, if I don't get finished too late, I could come over. We could at least go for a walk on the beach."

"I'd like that."

Peter escorted me to the door. We clung to each other, neither of us wanting our time together to end. His absence left such a deafening void. I knew I needed something to do to help me pass the hours until I heard from him again. Desperately hoping he truly would get hold of me when he finished work, I showered, got dressed, and went for a walk in Waikiki. It wasn't long before I saw the cutest dress and shorts outfit in the ABC store. My only thought was, *I must have them to wear for Peter.*

While grabbing a quick bite to eat, I counted my money. My heart dropped seeing how little I had left. I'd have to go get a job or find a less expensive place to stay soon.

I was tired. I got into my nightgown and decided to go to sleep early. This way I'd be fresh and rested for Peter—whenever he happened to return.

I awoke to a soft knock on the door. "Who is it?" I called, hoping it was Peter.

"It's me."

I opened the door and nearly fell into his arms. "What time is it?" I asked, enjoying the warmth of his embrace.

"It's two in the morning. I didn't get done as early as I'd hoped, but I just couldn't go home without seeing you. Let's go for a walk on the beach."

I left him sitting in a chair near the door while I dashed into the bathroom to change clothes. When I returned, he was asleep. "Are you sure you want to go for a walk?" I asked, waking him with a touch. "I think you need to go home and go to bed."

"I'm all right." He took me by the hand as he grabbed a blanket off the bed.

The night was awesome, with countless stars and the moon sparkling on the ocean. We walked silently for a long time. After a while, Peter spread out a blanket, lay down on his back, and pulled me down beside him. Our kisses were more passionate than they'd ever been before, and despite my deep attraction to him, I pulled away as horrible memories of those awful men flooded my mind.

Puzzled, he immediately apologized. "I'm sorry, Lyndie. I just can't help it. I want you so bad. I want to be with you all the time. I've never felt this way about anyone before."

Wanting to answer, to offer an explanation, I swallowed, not knowing what to say. Silently we held one another until we both drifted off to sleep.

The next thing I remember was Peter's anxious voice. "Lyndie, come on, wake up! Your skin feels like it's on fire." I opened my eyes and saw Peter looking down at me, the fear in his voice mirrored in his eyes.

Almost immediately I began shaking. My teeth chattered, and I could barely speak. "I'm fr—freezing," I said, knowing how ridiculous it sounded as we lay there under the blazing sun.

Peter quickly wrapped me in the blanket, lifted me off the sand, and carried me to his car.

"I shouldn't have let you get so cold and fall asleep last night."

"Whe—where are we go—going?"

"I'm taking you to the emergency room."

I did my best to control my chattering teeth as I protested, "But I don—don't have insurance."

"Don't worry. I'll take care of it."

The doctor in the emergency room diagnosed me with pneumonia and gave Peter prescriptions and instructions for me. When we stopped at the drugstore to get the medication, Peter went in while I waited in the car. He came back, not only with the medicine but with my favorite black cherry soda and chocolate covered cherries.

"Sweets for my sweet lady," he said, his smile slightly strained. I knew then he was more concerned about me than he let on.

Peter didn't leave my side for three days. He fixed me soup and put cool washcloths on my forehead. He even washed and brushed my hair. On the second day I tried to get up. I told Peter I needed to go to the office and pay for another week, but he wouldn't let me out of bed. He said he'd go down and make the payment for me. When I tried to give him the money, he put up his hand and said, "I've got this. I'm taking care of you, remember? By the way, who's Sam? You called out to him in your sleep."

I opened my mouth, not sure how to answer, then gave up and closed it again. Thankfully, Peter didn't pursue the issue.

On the afternoon of the third day, I began feeling better, but when I took a close look at Peter, I realized he was worn out.

"Go home," I ordered, willing my voice to be firm. "Get some rest before you get sick too."

I could see the arguments playing over his face, but then he relaxed and nodded. "Ok, baby. But call me if you need anything, you hear?" He kissed me on the cheek. "I'll call you later."

A few days went by with no call from Peter. I'd misplaced his business card and was nearing panic mode when the phone finally rang.

"Hi, baby. How are you?"

I ignored his question. "Are you okay? I've been worried."

"I'm sorry. I'm fine now. I guess I just caught what you had. I've been sick as a dog since I saw you last."

"I really apologize, Peter. I never meant for you to get sick."

"Of course, you didn't. Are you doing better?"

"Yes, I really am. I rested all day yesterday just to make sure."

"Great." His voice changed then. "Listen, I have some things to check on today at my business. I'll be there extremely late. Why don't we spend the day together tomorrow? I'd like to continue showing you around the island—as long as you're feeling up to it, of course. Plus, I have a surprise for you."

"I'd love to," I answered quickly. "But what's the surprise?"

He chuckled. "You realize it wouldn't be a surprise if I told you, right?"

"You're right. Okay. And I really do love surprises. I can't wait!"

Since Peter and I weren't going to spend the day together, I decided to go have my hair and nails done. I had gone to the front desk to pay my bill only to be pleasantly surprised to learn from the desk clerk my room had been paid for through the end of the month. Thanks to Peter. How would I ever find the words to thank him?

After persuading me to put red highlights in my auburn hair, the hairdresser gave me a cute, layered style for my shoulder length hair. I'd never had anything done to my hair, except for the bleached mess Carol had given me. Now I looked fabulous.

Sitting comfortably near a window in Cocoas facing the entrance, I noticed what appeared to be the perfect television family come in—mother, father, two children, and an older gentleman, perhaps a grandfather. My heart ached with deep longing for my parents, brother, and Sam while watching this family happily interacting with one another. The grandfather reminded me of Sam, with the same gentle eyes.

Overcome with emotion, tears welled up in my eyes. Oh, my! *What have I done to my family and Sam?* They must be frantic with worry. The urge to call them pricked my heart, but I hesitated. *I'll wait and tell Peter all about them,* I reasoned, and *then we can call them and go home to them together.* I'm just not ready yet. If I tell Peter about my family, I've got to tell him everything else too.

I swallowed. I loved Peter, and somehow, I knew he'd understand. *Then why was I so afraid to bring up the topic?* My shoulders slumped. I knew the answer. I'm afraid he'll think me dirty and used up. *What if he no longer respects me and walks out of my life?* I'll wait. Once I'm certain he loves me enough to spend the rest of his life with me—no matter what—then I'll tell him everything, I promised myself.

Leaving enough money on the table to cover my bill and a tip, I hurried from the restaurant out into the warm, sweet air. I am so selfish. *How can I ever face my parents or Sam?* I can't lose the magic I've found with Peter, and if I tell him my story, that's exactly what might happen.

Desperately needing to get my mind on something else, I stopped at the ABC Store and purchased a brochure of places to see on Oahu. I might as well educate myself about this island and maybe find some places I want Peter to take me.

After browsing the brochures, I went to bed early to be well rested when Peter arrived, but I couldn't quiet my mind from the thoughts of my family and Sam. All through that night, I dreamt of Sam and Sandy. I'd just finished showering the next morning when I heard Peter at the door.

"Just a minute," I called, quickly applying some mascara and blush, then wrapping a robe around me.

"Hi, beautiful," he said as I pulled the door open. "You look radiant." He swooped me up and swung me around, then lowered me gently as we embraced.

"I've missed you so much," I smiled, gazing up into those gorgeous blue eyes.

"Not as much as I missed you. You're in my thoughts constantly. Lyndie, you have my heart in the palm of your hand." He pulled back and grinned. "Now hurry and get dressed. I'm starving!"

We stopped for breakfast, and Peter got a double order of blueberry pancakes. I showed him the brochures I'd picked up, while he shoved bites into his mouth as he excitedly talked about our itinerary for the day.

We started at the Aloha Tower, then on to Iolani Palace, which I loved. I learned a great deal about the islands that day. I'd never realized Hawaii was the only state that had a ruling king and queen. As I continued to soak up the island's history, we drove to Pearl Harbor. We took the tour, and I was deeply touched when the guide told us the brave men who died at Pearl Harbor were still entombed in the Arizona at the bottom of the ocean.

The soberness of Pearl Harbor was replaced by a yummy lunch at Patti's Chinese Kitchen and a fun time at Sea Life Park. Especially getting splashed by the whales. Yet, even as beautiful a day it was and spending time just the two of us at the ocean, my mood dampened watching the children enjoying their time on field trips.

Peter interrupted my thoughts. "Do you like children?"

His words caught me off-guard as I thought of my younger brother, Tommy. He was a little boy when I was kidnapped, and it pained my heart to think how I'd missed seeing him grow up.

Peter must have noticed the tears in my eyes. He took my hand and quickly changed the subject. "Let's get some ice cream." I was grateful he didn't bring up the subject of children again that day.

As we left Sea Life Park, we noticed a TV crew filming Hawaii Five-0. We pulled over and got out of the car to watch. One of the cameramen approached us and asked if we'd want to be extras in the show.

Peter and I looked at each other, grinned, and immediately agreed. As it turned out it was thrilling to be part of the show, though our only part was to walk slowly down the beach, hand-in-hand.

"Wow!" I exclaimed as we drove away. "We were on Hawaii Five-0."

From that day on, Peter and I saw each other daily for the next couple of months. Then one day after snorkeling at Hanauma Bay, he announced, "Now, pretty lady, it's time for an incredibly special night on the town. First we're going to get you out of this snorkeling gear and into some appropriate clothes for this magical night."

"Is it okay if I shower at your hotel before we go?" he asked. "I want us to look absolutely amazing for this special night."

Peter showered first. While I took my turn, he excused himself to go get something—"a surprise" was all he said.

I'd just finished my hair and make-up when Peter returned, carrying the most beautiful purple orchid lei I'd ever seen. As he put it around my neck, he lightly brushed my lips with his. It was apparent I was in for the most memorable night of my life.

"Where are we going?" I asked as we headed out.

"Remember? It's a surprise."

In moments we arrived at the beautiful Outrigger Hotel. As we entered the lobby, Peter turned to me and flashed a saucy smile. "You ready for your first luau?"

My heart nearly burst, as I had always wanted to participate in this rich Hawaiian tradition.

An exotic Hawaiian girl placed a lei on Peter, then handed him one for me. "You put this on your lady," she instructed with a smile.

Placing a second lei around my neck, Peter kissed my lips and took my hand. In moments we were seated directly in front of the stage. The room grew dark, and the spotlights illumined the stage. Beautiful Hawaiian girls began to dance the hula, explaining the meaning of each hand movement, as some Hawaiian men joined the dance and told a story of the islands. Their fire dance, complete with flaming torches, was breathtaking. During intermission they asked if anyone would like to come up and learn to do the hula. Mostly young girls went up, but I hesitated even as Peter urged me to join them. I finally agreed, feeling awkward at first, but soon relaxed as I noticed how graceful it felt to do the hand movements.

Peter squeezed my hand as I returned to my seat. "You're a real natural. We need to put you in a hula dance class." I smiled at him, my heart singing, as the show continued.

⮜ 8 ⮞

Is This Love?

At the end of the show, Peter whispered in my ear, "Let's go for a walk on the beach."

I took his hand. "I'd like that. The ocean is so beautiful at night."

We took off our shoes and headed towards the shoreline. The water felt cool and refreshing on my feet. We journeyed silently for about a quarter of a mile down the beach, clinging to one another as we walked enjoying the fresh salty smell of the sea. The only sound was the rumble of the surf. Then the swell would hit the beach with a resounding crash before washing back into the rolling ocean.

It was Peter who broke the silence. "Ready for your surprise now?"

I grinned. "I thought the luau was my surprise."

"That was one of your surprises." I watched his eyes widen, his breathing quickening, and a silly grin spread across his face. "My parents live on Kauai in the town of Hanalei. I haven't visited them in some time now, and I'm thinking about taking a vacation to go see them. But I'm not going anywhere without you."

I felt my own eyes widen then. "Oh, Peter, meet your parents?" I clapped my hands in excitement and even jumped up and down. "I would love to!" And then silent words in my mind checked my excitement. *Meet his parents? What if they find out what you've done?* The mocking voice continued. *They're going to think you're dirty when they know the truth about you.* Suddenly I wasn't too excited about meeting his family, but I countered the doubts with reassuring words to myself. *He wants me to meet his parents. That's serious. He does love me!*

"You'll adore my folks," Peter said. "They're typical local people—welcoming, loving, and full of fun. My mother is Hawaiian-Japanese, and my dad is a Haoli."

"What's a Haoli?"

"That's what local people call a Caucasian person. But actually, he's lived here so long he's considered a local now. Also, you're going to love Kauai. It's the most beautiful of all the Hawaiian Islands."

"More beautiful than Oahu? I can't even imagine anything more magnificent than this."

"Just wait, lovely lady. Just wait!"

The next day Peter took me shopping. "You need some luggage for our trip," he explained, picking out a pink Samsonite bag and train case. "Pink is your color, Lyndie."

I hugged him. "Thank you so much."

Three days later Peter picked me up in a taxi and headed for the airport. I could barely contain my excitement as we boarded the small plane. A well-dressed Japanese family of three sat in the row between the captain and Peter and me. The captain and family chatted to each other in Japanese, and I noticed that when they said something to the captain, they bowed their head.

A sign of respect, I imagine. I looked out the window at the cumulous clouds hanging in the sky. They looked like huge cotton balls. My heart raced through the entire twenty-nine-minute flight, and kicked into overdrive when we landed.

We hadn't even deplaned when I began bombarding Peter with questions about my appearance and if he thought his parents would like me.

Peter put his arm around me as we stood in the aisle, waiting for the door to open. "Relax, Lyndie. They'll love you because I do."

Is This Love?

I gasped inwardly. *Oh, my, he does love me!*
While departing the small aircraft, I spotted a delightful-looking couple waving at Peter.

"There's my parents," he said, taking my arm and steering me toward them.

His mother, Noelani, was dressed in a cute Hawaiian print dress with muted blue colors. His father, James, whom his mother renamed Kimo (the Hawaiian name for James) when they started dating, was dressed in khaki shorts and a surfer shirt. Both were tanned and healthy looking. Neither looked old enough to have a son Peter's age.

After smothering Peter with kisses, Noelani grabbed me in a bear hug. "Ho'onani e komo mai. Welcome to our island home."

"So, here's the little lady who has captured my son's heart," Peter's dad observed before giving me a bear hug. He then put his hands on my shoulders and looked right into my face. "Lyndie, we are honored that you came to visit us." He smiled and winked at Peter before we all headed for the car.

Traveling from the small airport in Lihue to their home in Hanalei, Noelani chatted on about how she and Kimo had met when he was in the army. "I was visiting my cousin Malia on Oahu, and we went to a dance at Scofield Barracks. I walked to a table to get some punch and accidentally bumped into Kimo. He was so gracious when I apologized, but all I could think of was he was the handsomest man I ever saw. All night I wanted to talk to him, but I was shy. Several times I noticed him looking at me, but neither of us made a move. The next day Malia and I went to the beach, and Kimo was there."

She paused briefly and went on. "He immediately came over to me and said, 'Hey, aren't you the cute girl who bumped into me last night?' The next thing you know, we sat on the beach talking all day. When it was time to leave, he asked when he'd see me again, and I told him whenever he wanted. From that day on, we were inseparable. Kimo and I fell in love, and

63

he never left the islands." She went on to fill me in about Peter's boyhood in paradise, pointing out the spots where Peter learned to surf.

The A-frame house where Kimo and Noelani lived was amazing. A covered porch surrounded the house, which overlooked Hanalei Bay. The wood floors were made from old railroad ties Kimo got when they stopped running the sugarcane train on Kauai. He sanded them and polished them with a resin, and they were lovely.

Then Noelani pointed out a shelf near the ceiling of the living/dining area, which went all around the room. "This is where I put the shells, rocks, glass bottles, and other treasures from our walks on the beach."

At Noelani's invitation I sat in one of the wicker chairs with turquoise slipcovers while she shared each valuable find with me. After seeing most of them, I commented, "I'd love to collect things like this."

Noelani smiled. "You can, my dear. Every day brings a new treasure to discover from the ocean."

I looked out the panorama of windows and listened to the roar of the Pacific Ocean.

"Wait until you see the glorious sunset we get here," Kimo commented. It was hard to imagine the view being any more beautiful than it was at that moment.

Noelani wouldn't accept any help from me in preparing the food, giving me a chance to relax as she put together quite a spread. There were pineapples, mangos, guavas, passion fruit, and kiwi mixed in a salad with vanilla yogurt. We ate shrimp and fresh veggies, along with the fruit and yogurt, and Kimo opened a bottle of champagne.

———•———

After we finished eating, Kimo took Peter for a ride to show him the new horses he'd purchased for the ranch they owned not far from their home. While they were gone, Noelani offered to take me to her favorite beach for a walk. "So we can get better acquainted," she said.

I smiled. "Maybe we can find some treasures."

Noelani drove us to a secluded beach she called Lumahai Beach. "This is where the movie South Pacific was filmed."

"It's breathtaking," I whispered.

Two other people and a dog played in the water. Otherwise, the beach was vacant.

Noelani pulled two empty Ziploc bags out of her pocket and handed me one. "Let's gather shells," she suggested.

We'd barely begun our treasure hunt when she picked up a little, almost perfectly round shell with a hole in it. "This is a Puka shell. Puka means hole in Hawaiian. You can make necklaces and bracelets with these."

In about an hour our bags bulged with Puka shells. "Tell me about your folks, Lyndie. Where are you from?"

Her question caught me off guard. My whole body tensed with a heaviness in my limbs. I held my breath, wanting to run away. And yet despite my uneasiness, I knew I needed to respond. "They ... live in Maryland. I haven't seen them in a long time."

Silence followed, and I imagined Noelani must have noticed me blinking away tears. "Oh, I'm so sorry about that," she said. "It's time we head back to the house."

We found Peter and his dad on the back porch when we returned from the beach. Kimo was firing up the barbecue, while Peter gave me a gentle hug and kiss. Taking a second look at me, he asked, "What's wrong?"

Noelani shot him a cautioning look, shaking her head. "Why don't you go shower and freshen up for dinner, dear?" she suggested.

I breathed a sigh of relief. "Sounds like a good idea. Thanks."

I collapsed in the shower, pulling my knees up to my chin and wrapping my arms around my legs. Sobbing I let the warm water run over me. I wished it could wash away all the horrible memories from all the awful things I'd been forced to do. The thought of my family brought an even deeper pain. *What have I done, leaving them hanging, waiting for my long-awaited return?* And my dear sweet Sam. *What must he be thinking of me?*

A gentle knock on the door interrupted my thoughts. "Honey, dinner's almost ready."

Quickly I jumped out of the shower and splashed cold water on my eyes to get rid of any puffiness. I dressed in a pretty pale blue dress Peter had bought me for the trip, and it lifted my spirits as new clothes always seemed to do. I applied light makeup and pulled my hair up in a shell clip I'd purchased in Waikiki. Pushing away all thoughts of my family, I felt like Scarlett O'Hara as I said to myself, *I can't think about that now. If I do, I'll go crazy. I'll think about that tomorrow.* After all, tomorrow is another day.

⁓9⁓

Marry Me

After dinner Peter grabbed me by the hand. "Let's hurry down to the beach for the sunset." In moments we were enjoying the solitude as we watched the sun dip below the horizon, the waves mirroring the vibrant colors of the sky.

"With all this beauty, how could anyone deny the existence of God?" I reflected. As the words fell from my lips, I experienced the same warmth that had enveloped me the day I prayed with Sam. My mind drifted back the to the time this man of faith shared how much God loved me.

"Lyndie. Lyndie!" Peter's voice brought me back to the present. "Sometimes, my love, you seem a million miles away."

"No, just thinking," I answered, trying to cover my nervousness with a giggle, wondering why his hand seemed to be trembling.

He smiled. "About me, I hope."

Before I could answer, he bent down on one knee, still holding my hand.

My free hand flew to my mouth and I felt my eyes widen, but I didn't say a word.

"I never felt this way about anyone before," he said. "You're the love of my life. I've loved you from the moment I laid eyes on you on the plane. Right then I knew I could never be far away from you. We've only been together for a little over six months, but I'm going to be thirty next year, and I know what I want for my life. I want you to be my wife, and I want to take care of you and protect you. I know you've been hurt in the past, but I want to make you happy now and forever."

I couldn't speak. This must be a dream. I stared at Peter. This wonderful man wants to spend the rest of his life with me. But what if he knew the truth about me? The unspeakable things men did to me ...

"Say yes and make me the happiest man in the whole world," Peter urged, interrupting my negative thoughts.

Time stood still in the magic of the moment. The salty wind whipped my hair around my face. I'll never forget the eager look on Peter's face or the joyousness in my heart.

"Yes, yes!" I blurted, dispelling any agonizing warnings as Peter swept me up in his arms and twirled us around in the sand.

"Oh, wait!" He stopped and set me down. "I got so excited when you agreed to be my wife that I forgot this." He reached into his pocket and handed me a black velvet box.

With trembling hands, I opened it. The most exquisite white-gold pear-shaped diamond ring glistened in the middle of the box. "Oh, Peter," I gasped, unable to say more.

He slid the ring onto my finger, but it was too large. "We can get this sized to fit," he said, as he pulled me close. "Now let's go tell my parents."

Kimo peered into our faces. "Hey, something going on with you folks?" He turned then. "You'd better come here, Noelani," he hollered. "You need to see these kids."

Noelani hurried in from the kitchen. "Is something wrong?"

Peter and I giggled. "Well, you two, out with it! What's going on?"

Putting his arm around my waist and pulling me close, Peter said, "Lyndie has made my dreams come true today." He glanced at me and back at his parents. "She's agreed to become my wife."

Tears welled up in Noelani's eyes as she threw her arms around us. "Peter, I already love her like a daughter. She'll give you many little keikis."

Kimo took both my hands and gazed into my eyes. "You've

made my son incredibly happy today. We always wanted the best for Peter. I think he's found it in you." A tear glistened in his eye as he smiled. "Welcome to our family, my dear. Now can we please have our dessert and coffee?"

We all laughed as I showed off my ring to my future in-laws. All I could do for the rest of the evening was smile. I couldn't remember ever having been this happy.

While we enjoyed our dessert, Noelani rattled on about fixing up the ranch house for Peter and I to live in. I wasn't really listening. I was too busy looking at my Peter. By the time we were all ready to turn in for the night, my face hurt from smiling.

Peter walked me to my room. "Did you hear my mom talking about us living here?"

"You mean, here on Kauai? Oh, Peter, I love Hanalei. But how would you work? What about your business on Oahu?"

"I could still maintain my business and travel there weekly to check on things. Actually, my father has wanted me to run the horse ranch for a long time. He's ready to retire. I think we'd be happy here. It would be a good thing to be close to my family, especially when we have children. This is a great place to raise a family."

"Whoa, Peter," I cautioned with a grin. "Let's not get ahead of ourselves. We have time for that."

———•———

The following morning, I awoke to Noelani's voice calling to me through the door. "Come on, sleepyhead. We have lots to do today."

Rubbing my eyes, I walked into the kitchen and found Noelani already dressed and ready to go. "Peter and his dad already left for the ranch early this morning. He instructed me to let you sleep in since you had quite a day yesterday."

"How sweet of him." I yawned and stretched.

"Yes, but it's already ten-thirty, and Anake Aneala is waiting for us."

"Who? And why is she waiting for us?" I looked for coffee, anything to help the body wake up.

Noelani threw her hands up in the air. "Peter's aunt. She's a seamstress, the best in all the islands. People come from all over for her bridal gowns. She can customize any design from a bridal magazine to fit a bride's preference."

I gave up looking for caffeine. Noelani was obviously on a mission.

"We're stopping at her home first before we go to the flooring and furniture stores in Lihue," she explained.

"Okay, I'll hurry and get ready." I rushed into the bedroom, took a quick shower, tied my wet hair up in a ponytail, and dressed in white shorts and a black tank top. When I returned to the kitchen, Noelani already had her purse on her arm.

"Ready to go," I said, as I grabbed an apple out of the bowl on the kitchen counter.

"Don't worry about breakfast. We can stop at Starbucks on our way."

Throughout the drive Noelani jabbered on about the wedding, obviously at least as excited about it as I was. Grabbing two chai lattes and two old fashioned crumb cakes, we ate on the way.

Anake Aneala, which I soon learned means angel, was a round, cheerful woman with big brown eyes, and she hugged me so tight it hurt. Then she ushered us into her sewing room. Along the back wall I saw a rectangular table with all sorts of bridal fashion magazines.

"Look through these and decide what design you'd like for your wedding dress," she instructed. "And here are some samples of different fabrics you might like."

I was astonished at the many choices: laces, eyelets, silks, and satins. I danced from fabric to fabric, touching them to my skin. I went through page by page of each bridal magazine. I tried to match the dresses I liked with my choices of fabric. Then I closed my eyes and imagined myself in each dress. While I went back and forth with my choices, Anake Aneala made a pot of white ginger tea and brought out a plate of almond cookies. The two of them went and sat on the lanai, sipping tea and talking as I continued to flip through the pages of each magazine.

Several hours later, I fell madly in love with two designs. The first featured a strapless empire-waist dress with a bodice overlaid with antique lace. The second emphasized a long flowing skirt with layers of silk.

I walked out to the patio, "I picked out what I like."

"Let's see them!" Noelani rose from her chair.

"You've made some lovely choices, Lyndie," Anake Aneala said. She quickly sketched out a bridal gown. "See, I can combine those designs to create your dream wedding dress. I'll be right back."

Noelani added, "It's going to look fabulous on your petite figure."

"I brought this silk back from my last trip to Japan. I knew that someday I'd be using it for a bride's dress—for someone special."

"Oh, Anake, I adore it," I cried, throwing my arms around her. "It's the loveliest material I've ever seen. Please accept my deepest thanks."

After we said goodbye to Anake Aneala, Noelani and I drove to Lihue.

"Let's go into the flooring store."

"Okay."

"Peter told me he'd like to pull up the carpet in the front room and put in bamboo hardwood floors."

"Oh, I like the bamboo too, Noelani."

Our next stop was a furniture store. "Peter told me to have

you pick out several items that you like. Then the two of you will return together to make a final decision."

"So many choices. I like the leather sets but can't decide between the dark brown or burgundy. Which color do you prefer, Noelani?"

"Either would complement your ranch décor. Check out this maple coffee table. It would look good with either one of the couches."

I was happy about Peter's plan to help me with choosing our furniture. Such decisions should be made together as a couple, and besides, there were so many pieces I liked. There's no way I could have decided these details on my own.

On the way back to their house, Noelani said, "Kimo and I think, now that you and Peter are engaged, you should have more privacy. So, if you folks would like to, you can stay at the ranch house. Since Peter wants to be the one to redo the floors, he'll be right there to work on them."

When we returned, Kimo was busy cooking Teriyaki chicken and rice. Peter looked exhausted. I hugged him and whispered, "I love you."

Noelani babbled on all during supper about Anake Aneala, the dress, the floors, and the furniture. Peter smiled and gently squeezed my hand.

"It sounds like you had an exhausting day too. Let's have a glass of wine and turn in early," Peter spoke quietly later while driving.

We stepped into the house. Before turning on the light, Peter pulled me close. His warm lips met mine, and my body melted into his. Several heated seconds went by. My skin sizzled and I frantically pulled away.

The concern was evident in his voice. "Lyndie, what's wrong? You're going to be my wife soon."

I swallowed. "Peter, please understand. I want everything to be perfect on our wedding day. I want to wait."

He paused, "I don't know if I can. I want you to be all mine."

"Please, Peter. This is important to me."

He sighed. "Okay, sweetie. Why don't you relax on the couch? I'll be there in a minute with some wine. Then he opened a bottle of Zinfandel. Sitting down next to me, he handed me a glass and lifted his own. "To us," he said, his voice husky with emotion. "The happiest couple in the world!"

The wine, sweet and warm, relaxed me and I longed to feel Peter's touch. As if he'd read my mind, he leaned down and his mouth covered mine. Before I knew it, we'd gone further than we should have. Peter pulled away this time.

"I'm sorry, Lyndie. I know how you feel, and I want to honor your wishes. I sure am glad there are two bedrooms in this house."

I smiled and nodded, then stood up to head for the bedroom. "Me too. Good night, Peter. I love you."

"Love you more," he said, standing up to kiss the top of my head.

Later, lying in bed, I could still feel Peter's touch. "Peter's wife! He really does love me," I whispered.

≈10≈

Planning

I awakened around six to the tantalizing smell of bacon cooking. Immediately I thought of Sam. Dear Sam and the wonderful breakfasts he made for me after I escaped, nearly starved by my captors. *I must contact him ... and my parents.* I'll call as soon as Peter and I are legally married. He loves me, and he'll understand why I hesitated to tell him the truth. Satisfied, I had the situation under control, I threw on a robe, brushed my teeth, washed my face, and walked out into the kitchen.

"Good morning," Peter said as he hugged me. "I thought I'd start the day by making my future wife breakfast. Meanwhile put on these old clothes my mom sent with us last night. You're going to be my helper today."

I was happy to oblige; excited about what lay ahead, we worked on our new home. By the time I returned to the kitchen, Peter had breakfast on the table—bacon, eggs, rice, homemade biscuits, and fresh squeezed pineapple juice. He even set out a vase with beautiful freshly picked flowers. During breakfast Peter shared his plan for renovating the ranch house. I could hardly wait to get started!

Kimo showed up to help right as we finished cleaning up the kitchen. "Dad's here to help." He and Peter moved all the furniture into the garage. The father-son team made quick work of the carpet removal.

Kimo came back the following day to help us lay the bamboo flooring in the front room. They worked on it most of the day, and when they were done, it looked fantastic.

"The bedrooms are smaller; they will go quicker."

74

"I know, Dad. Ripping out the carpet was the worst part of the job."

Several days later, more than ready for a relaxing break and a good meal, we headed over to have dinner with Kimo and Noelani. Peter's parents hugged us, "Why don't you folks go for a swim first? Dinner is not quite ready."

The salt water of the ocean was soothing to our aching bodies, and I floated on my back, looking up at the amazing sunset. My mind wandered back to God and how awesome His creation is.

Peter swam under me and lifted me up into his arms. "Come on, sweetheart, time to eat. I'm starving."

Peter took my hand as we walked together out of the water. He threw my beach towel around my shoulders and gave me a big bear hug to dry me off. We quickly used the outside shower and went inside to dress for dinner.

Noelani had made a big Greek salad, corn on the cob, and grilled Mahi Mahi. We were all ravenous and wasted no time digging in.

"Can I help you clean up, Noelani?"

"You two worked hard today. I can clean up. Take my son home and get some rest."

We kissed and hugged Peter's folks. I laid my head on Peter's shoulder and was almost asleep when he pulled into the driveway.

Peter gently shook me and said, "I'm beat, honey. I know you are too. Let's turn in."

The next morning, I woke up before Peter and decided to surprise him and cook a special breakfast. I made French toast with papaya and squeezed oranges to make fresh juice. As I was heating the maple syrup, Peter walked into the kitchen with a big grin on his face. His hands encircled my waist, and I looked up at him as he leaned down. His lips brushed my cheek, and I giggled. His touch sent shivers down my spine.

"Everything smells wonderful," he whispered, glancing at the stove.

"Sit down. You need a nourishing breakfast. We have lots of hard work to do today."

"Hi, you two. Your help has arrived." We laughed at Kimo who was decked out in white overalls with a tool belt hanging from his waist.

"Mind if I do," Kimo helped himself to a large helping of French toast.

The men worked on the bedroom floors while I painted.

Halfway through the afternoon, Noelani arrived with a platter of cold cuts, chicken wings, cheese, and Hawaiian sweet bread. She brought enough for us to have leftovers for dinner too.

Laughing, she looked at me, "It seems that my daughter painted herself along with the walls." I ran into the bathroom. Sure enough, my hair, face, and clothes were covered in paint. We worked on the house until well after dark.

Kimo yawned, "Wow! It's getting late. I'll be back in the morning. You two get some rest."

"I'm beat too," Peter admitted. "Our plan is to finish the guest room tomorrow."

While Peter showered, I warmed up wings, steamed some rice and vegetables. While Peter ate, I soaked in a hot lavender oil bath.

I'd been bathing for quite a while when Peter knocked softly on the door. "Hey, you didn't fall asleep in there, did you?" I assured him I hadn't and quickly got out of the tub and into my pajamas. When I emerged from the bathroom, I found Peter standing at the door holding a glass of wine for me.

"Want to sit on the porch awhile? There's a full moon."

As tired as I was, I couldn't pass up an invitation like that. "Sure. Sounds great."

Peter sat close to me on the porch swing as we enjoyed the stillness of the night. After a few minutes he put his arm around me and asked, "What are you thinking about, my darling?"

"How happy you've made me."

I watched his face light up in the moonlight. "I want to spend the rest of my life making you happy." Then he kissed me, gently at first, then with more passion. This time both of us stopped before things went too far.

"Come on, Lyndie," he said. "We'd better go to bed and rest. I need to regain my strength to finish the work on this house. And tomorrow you have wedding planning to complete, don't you?"

———•———

The following week, Peter and Kimo finished the last of the floors, and I completed the last touch up painting of the kitchen.

"Noelani, I love the way the cabinets have a glass front; you can see the dishes inside."

She smiled and nodded. "Yes, and you'll have pretty china to put in there. We need to hurry, though. It's one-thirty, and your appointment with the florist is at two-thirty."

The owner of the florist shop showed me different wedding bouquet arrangements and let me smell various flowers. "I really like this design," I told her. "It's simple. And I'd like it to have gardenias and small yellow roses with a white satin bow."

The wedding photographer, Dan, was awesome. "I think since your ceremony is on the beach," he said, "we should definitely use the ocean as the backdrop." He showed me photos of several other weddings he had photographed. "I love this one, Dan, with the sunset right behind the bride and groom as they are kissing. That's one of my favorites. Kimo's brother promised to video tape. And now we'll have an album too."

A delivery truck was at our house when we got home. "I'm delivering the antique oak cabinet and claw tub you ordered." Early the next day, Peter and Kimo ripped out the bathroom appliances to install them. They worked well into the evening. Sweaty and dirty, Kimo announced, "I'm going home to shower. Noelani and I would like to take you folks to dinner at Charley's Steak House."

"Yummy, you'll love it there, Lyndie." Dinner was wonderful. Noelani chatted on about the wedding. Peter interrupted, "Hey, let's go to the furniture store together tomorrow, Lyndie, to pick out what we want for our new home. The floors and all the other renovations should be done by the time they deliver our furniture."

After Peter's parents dropped us off at the ranch house, Peter picked me up in his arms and carried me inside.

I laughed. "What are you doing?"

"I'm practicing for our wedding night."

"Okay, Bud, but that's far enough," I reminded him as he headed for the master bedroom.

"I was just playing," he laughed, putting me down. "I was going to toss you on the bed. But okay, you win. Good night, my love." He gave me a quick kiss and disappeared into the guest bedroom.

When I climbed into bed, I kept hearing Peter's words. Our wedding night. The thought brought a cold fear into my heart. *What if Peter can tell I've been with all those men? What if my insides are damaged thanks to what was done to me, and I can't have children?* I pushed the feelings away, and sleep soon overtook me.

We stopped for breakfast on our way to the furniture store. I took a sip of coffee and looked at Peter. "Honey, we haven't set a date for our wedding."

"I thought it was understood that we'd get married as soon as the house and your dress were ready."

"Oh." It was my turn to be perplexed. *Why would he assume that?*

His brow furrowed. "That's what you want, right?"

I want to get married, but ... I searched his face. This man really does love me. *How can I say no to him? More importantly, though, am I ready?* Things seemed to be moving too fast. *But I do love him...*

"Of course, I do," I finally managed to say.

Later we strolled hand-in-hand into the furniture store. I hadn't told Peter which furniture I'd picked out, and I hoped he'd like the same sets I chose. As it turned out he picked out a large, dark brown modern leather sectional.

"Peter, that set is much too big for the living room. Don't you think it'll make the room look dark?"

"I like it," he answered matter-of-factly. "It gives us lots of room for company. And look over here. This oak coffee table would fit perfect with it."

Feeling defeated I sat down. Peter noticed my disappointment. "Lyndie, I'm sorry. I guess I'm used to getting my way. This is our first home. We need to agree on this together. Show me what you liked."

I bolted out of the chair. "I thought this burgundy Gypsum leather sofa and chair would go great with our ranch theme."

"You're right! The rounded arms are classy too. I like it. The color would brighten up the room. But I'm not real fond of the table you picked out to go with it. How about we try the oak instead?"

"This is perfect, Peter. I think we have a good match here." Peter wrapped his arms around me. "Well, we resolved our differences and had fun doing it."

Before we left Peter found a unique wine rack and paid the salesman who promised delivery of the furniture in three to five days.

⁓11⁓

My Dream Comes True

"This is so exciting!" Auntie Anake clapped her hands. "Perfect! It fits you perfectly, and you look lovely in it. All that needs to be done is to add the antique lace on the bodice. Your dress will be ready soon."

Peter was ecstatic when I told him the news at lunch. "Wait 'til I tell my mom! She'll be beside herself when she learns she has only a week to get the flowers and food together."

In that moment I realized I was the one who wasn't ready. I was actually scared! I'd come to the realization that none of what I'd been through was normal. *How could I start my own family and pretend to be normal?* The voices from the past taunted me: *Girls like you never change.*

Without thinking I blurted out, "Don't put that kind of pressure on your mom. We can give her another week or so."

His eyes widened. "Wait longer than we have to? No way, Lyndie." He shook his head. "It's going to be the longest week of my life as it is."

I sighed and nodded. There was nothing I could do—unless I broke down and told him my entire story, which could mean losing him all together. I wasn't willing to take that chance.

We delivered the news to Noelani at her home later that afternoon. "Peter," she said, "we want this to be a perfect wedding for you and Lyndie, and she needs more time. I need to send out invitations and make phone calls. Not to mention that your father needs more time to finish his surprise wedding gift for you two."

Together, Noelani and I talked Peter into compromising. He

finally agreed to wait two weeks for the wedding. My shoulders relaxed.

"Did I hear someone mention my surprise?" Kimo called, slamming the door.

Noelani smiled and greeted her husband with a kiss. "Yes, dear. We were discussing the date for the wedding."

"Well, funny thing is, I just finished their gift. Why don't you folks come and see your surprise now? I still want to put another coat of shellac on it, but otherwise it's ready."

When we saw the surprise, I gasped, "This has to be the most charming gazebo I've ever seen."

Before I could thank him, Kimo said, "We can decorate the roof with flowers, and you folks can get married in it. Of course, we'll have to haul it down to the beach for the ceremony. Then after the wedding, we'll set it up in the backyard of your ranch house."

"Oh, how thoughtful of you, Kimo," I said, squeezing back the tears. "I am so grateful to you. It's beautiful!" Tears spilled over onto my cheek, as I hugged my soon-to-be father-in-law. I couldn't believe he'd made something so incredibly lovely for us. "It's amazing."

"Nothing's too good for my son and my delightful new daughter."

The phone rang. "It's Anake Aneala. She needs for you to come for a final fitting. She has added the lace to your dress. Peter will have to drive you. I still have to order the flowers and confirm the wedding singers."

"That's fine, Mom. We need to leave now. I have to run some errands in town. Don't forget, Lyndie, we have to make a stop at the jewelry store to get your engagement ring sized and pick out our wedding rings."

Peter's errands seemed unnecessary. After a while, I rolled my eyes and folded my arms. "Peter," I snapped, "you're wasting time. Hurry up. These things can wait." My agitation left when we entered Kay Jewelers. We were fortunate the jeweler was there and able to size my ring while we waited. Peter picked out a yellow gold band for me, with diamonds cut in that fit perfectly with my engagement ring. I picked out a white gold band for Peter, with a diamond chip in the middle of it.

"Since my ring isn't ready yet," Peter said, "let's walk around the mall and get something to eat."

"Look, Peter, see that cobalt blue aloha shirt?'

"Yeah."

"It would look great on you. It sure makes your eyes look even bluer."

"I like it too. Let's get it."

We sat down at some tables, enjoying a mango-strawberry smoothie and a veggie wrap.

"It won't be long before that's you," Peter winked at me with a grin, catching me off guard, as a pregnant lady with two toddlers walked by our booth. His smile faded briefly. "You want lots of children, don't you?"

I swallowed the lump in my throat. "Honey, it doesn't matter how many children we have. I just want them to be healthy and for you to be their father."

He leaned over and gave me a quick kiss on the cheek. "Let's go check on the rings."

Panic clutched at me as we walked. *It's really happening. I'm going to be Peter's wife. What if he sees right through me?* Once married I'll explain to Peter that I never wanted that kind of life, that it wasn't my choice. Yet the voices rang in my head: *You're trash! That's all you'll ever be—trash!*

I felt so dirty I could almost smell an odor about me. I worked hard convincing myself I was just having pre-wedding jitters, and everything would be all right. *Peter adores me,* I reminded myself.

Before we reached the jewelry store, I glanced at a dress hanging in the window at Francesca's. It was a lovely summer dress made of sheer chiffon, in different hues of blue.

"Hey, that would go with the Aloha shirt I just bought," he smiled. "Let's get it."

With the blue dress in tow, we returned to the jewelry store and found our rings were ready. Peter slipped my engagement ring on my finger. "Fits perfect," he said. Then he kissed me, and the other customers applauded. I was embarrassed, but I knew I had to get used to the fact that Peter was affectionate in public.

When we arrived at Peter's auntie's house, she told Peter, "You need to wait outside."

He raised his right hand. "I promise not to peek."

She gave him a playful smack on his head. "You know it's not good luck to see the bride in her gown before the wedding."

"We don't believe in superstitions."

She put her hands on her ample hips. "My house, and I'm telling you not to come in."

Peter sighed and went to wait in the car while I tried on my dress. I gasped at my reflection in the mirror. Not only was it the most beautiful dress I'd ever seen, but I couldn't believe I was the one wearing it! And then the voices in my head shouted, *You don't deserve to wear white. White is for women who are pure.* I put my hands over my ears. Nothing was going to spoil this moment for me.

After the fitting we went to Peter's parent's house, where we noticed an unusual number of cars on the road. Confused at the sight, Kimo rushed out the door and yelled to Peter, "Come, let's go to the ranch house. The furniture will be delivered tomorrow. We need to move the old furniture out. We can hang the new wooden blinds and put one more coat of sealer paint on the kitchen cabinets." Holding the passenger-side door open for me, he said, "Lyndie, Noelani needs your help inside." I got out. Kimo got in, and he and Peter drove away, leaving me to wonder why Noelani needed my help.

I stood just inside the front door, blinking in disbelief as I realized Peter's relatives, neighbors, and friends had come to honor me with a bridal shower. I opened my mouth but couldn't think of a thing to say. *How did they all get here so fast?* Even Anake Aneala was there! I looked around and saw the room was decorated with streamers of plumerias and balloons. Presents covered a card table, while another larger table was filled with finger sandwiches, guacamole and tortilla chips, and a big fruit salad.

I couldn't remember ever feeling this special. Everyone loved on me, and the presents would make a wonderful addition to our new home. Noelani got me a beautiful set of Noritaki china. I received a total of two hundred dollars in gift cards for Victoria's Secret, and one hundred dollars for Bed, Bath, & Beyond. The other gifts included three cute little negligees, underwear, satin slippers, and essential bath oils.

"How can I possibly thank you? I love and appreciate you having this shower for me. I never expected anything like this. What wonderful gifts. You made me feel cherished today."

"Why aren't any of your family here?" asked one of Peter's aunts.

Noelani sent her an annoyed look. I guessed she was one of the few my future mother-in-law had neglected to warn about not bringing up that subject.

My throat tightened, and my mouth went dry, but Noelani stepped in. "Lyndie's parents are unable to travel at this time."

My parents. Oh, how I've hurt them already, and now to not even have them at my wedding. How I'd love for my father to walk me down the aisle and my mother to be smiling through tears of happiness. Of course, I'd want Sam to be here too. Dear, sweet Sam, my friend and my rescuer ...

I knew Sam would have been overjoyed to see me wed, but I'd deeply hurt and disappointed them all.

Maybe after Peter and I are married, I'll have the courage to tell him about what I've been through and what I did to my parents and Sam. Then I can persuade him to come with me to see my parents and, yes, Sam too. With Peter by my side, I'll be braver.

Later that night in the relative safety of my room, I prayed my parents and Sam would be understanding when the time came. "Please, God," I whispered, "keep my mom, dad, Tommy, Sam, and Sandy well until I can go see them."

———•———

"Our furniture's here!" I sprang out of bed, quickly changed clothes, and rushed into the living room. Peter and the deliverymen were already setting up the couch.

"Oh! It's beautiful!" I cried. It took a bit of scrambling, but we managed to get everything set up. I looked around at how beautifully all the furniture fit into our ranch décor. "Wow Peter, it really feels like our home."

"It sure does, and we did this together."

I sighed and leaned into the man I loved. "Oh, Peter, you've made all my dreams come true."

He held me close but leaned back to look down into my eyes. "It's you, my darling, who've fulfilled my dreams."

I closed my eyes as he kissed me. All my anxious thoughts—about the wedding, about my parents, about Sam—disappeared in his embrace.

⮞12⮜

The Ceremony

The weather was perfect for a wedding on the beach—seventy degrees with a slight breeze.

Noelani's hairdresser put my hair up, with little tendrils hanging down on my cheeks. A lace veil decorated with yellow roses on the hem, perfectly matched my bouquet of gardenias and yellow roses.

Kimo decorated the gazebo with white and yellow plumerias. Noelani ensured that our wedding stayed true to the Hawaiian traditional food. Trays of all sorts of fruits, veggies, and salads covered a long table, along with Noelani's many baked goods. Kimo had roasted a Kalua pig in a pit in the ground, and the caterers had delivered Huli Huli chicken, Teriyaki beef, rice, and a beautiful three-tier carrot wedding cake with cream cheese frosting decorated with yellow plumerias.

As I nervously adjusted my veil, a soft knock on the door interrupted my thoughts.

"Come in," I called.

Noelani stepped inside and handed me a pink velvet box.

"What's this?" I asked.

She smiled. "Just something for your special day."

I gasped at the sight of a dainty string of pearls.

"These belonged to my mother," Noelani said as I lifted the pearls from the box and gently cradled them in my hand. "She gave them to me on my wedding day."

Overwhelmed, I rose to my feet and threw my arms around my almost-mother-in-law. "Oh, they're lovely! Thank you so much for your kindness, Noelani."

I bit my lip, hoping to stop the threatening tears. During my time in captivity, I never imagined anyone giving me such a special gift.

She grinned. "It's Mom now. I love you like a daughter, Lyndie." I nodded. "And I love you like a mother." As I spoke the word "mother," I felt a deep pain echo deep in my heart. *Oh, how I wish my own mother were here.* Tears shimmered in my eyes. "No tears, sweet girl. It's going to be okay." Music drifted in from the beach. "It's time!"

I slowly walked down the beach, feeling like a queen at her coronation. All eyes were on me, and I heard someone whisper, "She's such a lovely bride."

Peter's face lit up like it did the first time he saw me on the plane. His eyes never left mine as I walked toward him. Handsomely dressed in the traditional groom's Hawaiian attire, he wore a white shirt, white pants, and a yellow sash around his waist. A delicate white lei made of little white flowers called pikoki hung around his neck. Peter took my hand and squeezed it as I took my place by his side.

The ceremony was glorious. Pastor Stangel took a white cord and wrapped one end around Peter's hand, one around mine, and then tied the cords to a cross. "Peter and Lyndie, the Bible reminds us, 'Though one may be overpowered, two can defend themselves. A cord of three strands is not quickly broken.' If you stay tied to Jesus, your marriage will never fail." A chill ran down my body. *Peter. Oh, how I love him!* He's the first man to ever show me real love. He rescued me from my ugly past, and now he's making my future sunshine and roses.

We proceeded to braid God's Knot. Peter held a small metal ring with three different colored strands attached to it, as I braided the strands together.

Pastor Stangel continued. "The cord of three strands, God's Knot, represents the journey of one man, one woman, and God into a marriage relationship. The divinity of God is represented by the gold. This covenant relationship is initiated by him and will be built under his authority and is intended to glorify him. The husband is represented by the purple. As the husband loves his wife and submits himself to the Lord, the Lord, in turn, will demonstrate His great love in the marriage relationship. The white strand represents the bride who's been cleansed by salvation in Christ. The purity of the bride is represented in white. As the wife honors her husband and submits herself to the Lord, the Lord, in turn, will nurture and strengthen the marriage relationship."

The word pure echoed in my head. I'm anything but that.

"Before they take their vows, the bride and groom have some words they want to express to one another."

We turned and faced each other. Peter held my shaking hands as I gazed into his eyes.

"Lyndie, you're the person that keeps me singing, smiling, and laughing. When I look at you, I know how much God loves me because He gave me you as a gift. I will spend the rest of my life loving you. You are my treasure."

"Peter, you're my best friend, my forever, and an answer to prayer. When I look at you, I see a reflection of God's heart, how He pursued me and loved me, even when I didn't love myself. Your heart is my home, and your arms are my shelter."

After the exchanging of vows and rings, Pastor Stangel announced, "By the power vested in me, I now pronounce you husband and wife. Peter, you may kiss your bride."

Peter took my face in his hands, his eyes full of love. Our first kiss as husband and wife was tender but firm. Pastor Stangel motioned for us to turn and face Peter's family and friends. Mine, thousands of miles away, had missed my joyous day.

"I would like to introduce to you Mr. and Mrs. Peter Stanton."

"Mr. and Mrs. Peter Stanton," I whispered.

It was a delightful wedding reception in the backyard. I smashed cake into Peter's face, and everyone laughed. We danced and ate the afternoon away with many relatives and friends celebrating with us. Kimo clapped Peter on the back.

"You folks need to get going or you'll miss your plane."

Peter and I looked at each other, "What plane?"

Kimo grinned. "Your plane to Kona for the honeymoon. For your wedding gift, your mother and I arranged a five-day stay at the Four Seasons Resort Hualalai."

Shocked, but thrilled, we hugged his parents, thanked them, and said our goodbyes.

On the plane to the Big Island of Hawaii, I closed my eyes, nestled against Peter, reminiscing the first ride where we'd met and thanking God for my wonderful husband.

⸙13⸙

Not the Wedding Night We Planned

When we deplaned, another limo waited to take us to our hotel. The exquisite resort included everything we could possibly want for our honeymoon. We giggled with excitement when the front desk attendant told us to enjoy the Jacuzzi tub in the room, a complementary couple's massage, and a beautiful private beach.

After we checked in, Peter carried me into our room, held me close, and whispered in my ear, "You're my lovely wife now. I love you, Mrs. Stanton."

Our bed was covered with deep crimson rose petals. A chilled bottle of champagne sat on the table, along with a basket of cheese, crackers, fruit, and a box of dark chocolates shaped like wedding bells. An assortment of wines and champagne were also stocked in the refrigerator.

I went into the bathroom to change into a darling white satin negligee. After I was in there awhile, Peter rapped on the door.

"Hey, honey, come on out. I have a surprise for you."

The room glowed in the soft light of candles. Peter swooped me up in his strong arms and carried me to the bed, poured me a glass of champagne, and declared, "To us!"

"To us!" I giggled.

"Your surprise is under the pillow. It's my first gift to you as my wife."

"Another gift?" I grinned. "You're spoiling me, you know." I reached under the pillow and pulled out a small white box. Inside the box lay a sparkling diamond tennis bracelet.

"Oh, Peter, I love it!" I paused as my smile faded. "But I didn't get you anything."

He smiled suggestively. "Well, you can give me a gift right now." Then he gently lowered me down on the bed and began to caress my body. As his kisses grew more passionate, I stiffened and abruptly sat up.

"What's the matter, honey?"

"My ... my stomach hurts, and I'm feeling dizzy." It was a lie, but I couldn't bring myself to tell him the truth, not tonight on our honeymoon. "It must be all the champagne."

"It's okay. It's been a long day for both of us, and I'm pretty tired myself." He stood and gently kissed my cheek. "Hey, no problem. We have the rest of our lives together."

I smiled and nodded in relief, thankful Peter was considerate and didn't press the issue. When he began to make love to me, the awful memories of the things I'd been forced to do with so many men flooded my mind, and I became sick to my stomach. *But Peter loves me. Next time I'll just force myself to concentrate on him, and it will be all right.*

We turned the days of our honeymoon into adventures. Peter rented a 4WD, and we traveled to Waipi'o Valley. I was in awe at the beauty of the taro fields with the mountains as the backdrop. Wild horses frolicked on the beach, as Peter taught me to body surf. I laughed each time I got up and ran back to the surf to catch another wave. By early evening we returned to the Four Seasons Resort and enjoyed a romantic dinner by the saltwater lagoon, watching a myriad of tropical fish glide gracefully through the water. I was pleased we were exhausted after eating and fell asleep in each other's arms.

The rest of the week was full of fun and adventure. I marveled at the ocean as we sat on the beach enjoying the scent of salt air. We put our towels down on the fine white sand.

"Peter, look how deep blue the ocean is. What's that strange wailing sound?"

"That's a whale song. Look out there. If you watch closely, you might see them jumping out of the water."

A few seconds later we spotted one bursting upward. "Wow, what magnificent creatures."

We spent the rest of the afternoon snorkeling at Kuo Bay. Peter grabbed my hand as he pointed out the many colorful tropical fish in the reef.

"Look a Humuhumunuknukuapuaa!"

"A what?'

"It's the Hawaii state fish. It translates to a reef triggerfish with a snout like a pig."

"Listen Peter," I said giggling, "it's making grunting noises."

The fantastic beauty of the underwater world and the joy of floating on the warm tropical water made it a perfect day.

On our third day, we decided to hike Kilauea Iki trail in Hawaii Volcanoes National Park. We walked around the crater and through the lush rainforest. When the weather suddenly changed from warm and sunny to wet and windy, I was glad Peter had suggested we bring light raincoats.

Our honeymoon week ended much too quickly as we enjoyed a helicopter tour to some of the most amazing places on the island, which were extremely difficult to reach over land. The Kihala coast and the Waipi'o Valley, with more than 2000 cliffs and waterfalls, were breathtaking. Peter laughed as I clung to him, scared, when the pilot maneuvered the helicopter so close to the cliffs I could almost reach out and touch them and feel the spray from the thundering falls.

Without a doubt, the couples' massage therapy was a most delightful and relaxing treat before spending our last hours shopping and hanging out at the resort. Walking hand-in-hand with Peter through the shops brought a sense of pride through me. I'm really married! He's my husband, and I want so much to make him happy.

Although every day was full of fun, at night things were not so good. Each time Peter tried to make love to me, I told him to stop. It hurt so much due to all the physical damage that had been done to me from the multiple rapes. The images of those acts still haunted me, and I simply couldn't relax.

Peter was sweet and did everything he could to calm me and make me feel comfortable. "Things will be better when we're in our own home and bed, you'll see," he reassured me.

I hoped he was right, but when we arrived at home, things went from bad to worse. I found myself making excuses when it was time for us to be intimate. My heart ached to please my husband, but I just didn't see how that could ever happen.

$\approx 14 \approx$

Peter's Departure

After two weeks of listening to my excuses, Peter stormed out of the house and came home late, smelling of alcohol. I pretended to be asleep when he came into the bedroom, but he climbed on me roughly and declared, "You're my wife."

Without thinking I slapped him in the face, "Get off me!"

Peter fell off the bed, and I quickly climbed down onto the floor and wrapped my arms around him. "Baby, I didn't mean to hurt you," I sobbed. "I'm so sorry. I love you so much. You just scared me."

Peter stared at me angrily. "I've been as patient as I can be with you. I'm sick and tired of this!" He stomped out of the bedroom—the door slamming shut behind him.

I lay in bed sobbing, thinking about what I was doing to Peter. This isn't fair to him. I'm supposed to please my husband. Needless to say, I didn't sleep well. In the middle of the night, I awoke to find Peter sitting on the edge of the bed.

"I apologize," he said. "I shouldn't have left you alone and gone into the other room. I know you've been deeply hurt in the past. We need to work this out together."

I sobbed as he pulled me close.

"It's going to be all right, babe. I'm here. I won't let anyone harm you again."

We fell asleep in each other's arms, and the next day at breakfast, Peter insisted we go to counseling together. I said I would, but I was afraid the counselor would disclose all the molestations and horrible things I was forced to perform.

Two weeks later, anxious and uneasy, we attended our first

of several counseling sessions. Our counselor was calm and understanding. She counseled us separately. I was relieved my secret stayed hidden and didn't have to deal with the pain of what I'd been through. She focused on our marriage issues, rather than our individual issues. She suggested we go on little date adventures. Peter and I agreed the sessions helped, not solving our intimacy problems, but by bringing us closer.

The ranch kept us busy, and we often took long horseback rides together. Riding high up on the horse gave me a sense of childlike freedom I'd never experienced before.

I did all I could to be a good wife to Peter. I cooked his favorite meals and learned how to sew. For Peter's birthday I made him a shirt. I turned our house into a home, but though I did everything to please him, after a year we still had not consummated our love. I knew Peter wanted to have children, and I was concerned our marriage wouldn't survive.

On Father's Day, Noelani, Kimo, Peter, and I gathered for a midday meal. Nolelani had prepared meatloaf, mashed potatoes, green beans, and one of her husband's favorite desserts, pumpkin pie. I thought she made enough to feed the entire neighborhood.

"Everything smells delicious," I said while we were all in the kitchen.

"As you know, Mom is a great cook," Peter said.

She smiled and handed him a stack of plates. "Here. Set the table."

Peter took the dishes, and I followed him into the dining room. He set each of the four plates between the silverware already on the table. A bouquet of fresh-cut flowers sat in the center.

Peter's dad took his place at the head of the table, his mother at the opposite end, Peter to his dad's right, and me across from my husband. Noelani passed the potatoes to me. "When are you two going to give us some grandbabies?"

I took the bowl, glancing at Peter, who slumped a little in his chair. When neither of us replied, Noelani switched topics, asking Kimo when he thought he might repaint the barn.

"I don't know," he said, smiling and holding a large piece of meatloaf in front of his mouth. "Does the barn need painting?"

The room got noticeably quiet. When neither of us responded, Noelani had the insight to change the subject once again.

The rest of the day, Peter seemed preoccupied. He didn't say a word during dinner, even when I tried to make small talk. He grunted or nodded his head.

I helped Noelani clean up the kitchen. Peter made an excuse about feeling tired so we could leave. We didn't speak on the drive home.

When we walked into the house I said, "I'm going to take a shower."

Getting into bed I found Peter already asleep. I lay down next to the man I adored and wished I could be one hundred percent his wife. I knew Peter had tried to accept the way things were with us, but he was a man with needs, and I simply wasn't meeting them.

It wasn't long before I started doubting whether I should have married. How could he want someone who's done what I've done to be the mother of his children? It even crossed my mind to leave Peter. But I loved him too much. That was my answer. I told myself that if I truly loved him, I should want what's best for him, and that meant I need to not hurt him and to keep trying.

In my heart I felt I'd not only let him down, but I'd deceived him. Hiding secrets from the man I married was wrong. I must tell Peter everything. But … what if it changes his feelings and he leaves me? My fear of the truth of my past was destroying our marriage, and the voices in my head kept telling me how dirty and unworthy I was.

I opened my eyes the next morning to find Peter already dressed and packing a small bag.

I quickly sat up. "What's going on? What are you packing for?"

"I need to get back to Oahu and check on my business," he said without looking at me.

"I thought now that we're living here, you were just going to run the ranch."

"That's after the business sells."

"You told me you put it up for sale a while ago and had a prospective buyer."

He ignored my comment. "I'll be back in a few days. I need some time to sort things out. I've put a lot of demands on you lately. Now you'll have a break from me."

"I don't need a break from you."

"It'll be for the best. When I return, we'll have had time to miss each other."

I could see there was no way to persuade Peter not to leave. He gave me a brief hug and was gone. As he walked away, I felt like he was slipping out of my life forever. And I knew it was my fault.

Peter's mom called that afternoon to see if I wanted to go with her to lunch.

"I'm sorry, Noelani, I have a terrible headache," I replied.

"Okay, my dear," she answered, though I could hear the doubt in her voice. "I hope you feel better. Maybe tomorrow."

"I'll see how I'm doing then."

I suspected she knew Peter had left, and she didn't want me to be alone. She called the next two days, and I let the answering machine pick it up. Peter phoned only once to let me know he had arrived safely. I left three messages for him on his phone. When he didn't reply, I stopped trying to contact him.

On the fifth day, he called to tell me he'd have to be there for another week on business. Noelani showed up that afternoon and apologized for coming over unannounced. "Honey, I'm concerned about you. You look terrible."

I went into the bedroom to change out of my pajamas while she made coffee. Glancing at myself in the mirror, I realized Peter's mom was right. I did look awful. Dark circles under my eyes. Blotchy color. My hair was a mess, and my roots needed a touch-up.

"I know this is none of my business, but is everything okay with you and Peter?" Noelani asked while she sipped her coffee.

A dam burst inside me. I lay my head down on the table and sobbed. Being her typically kind self, Noelani didn't ask any other questions. "Come on, let's go have a day of beauty. You'll see that once you get a facial and a pedicure and get your hair done, you'll feel much better. We can even go shopping. I'd love to buy my daughter a new outfit."

Once I'd stopped sobbing, I nodded. "It'll probably do me good to get out of the house."

On the way to town, Noelani confided in me, "The first year of a marriage can be difficult. Early in my marriage, Kimo went home to his mother's twice. I went to him with an ultimatum...come home to your wife!" Her confession helped me see that they worked things out, and it gave me hope for Peter and me. "Noelani, I appreciate how much you love me and want to not only make me feel better but give me hope for my marriage."

Noelani bought me a cute yellow pants outfit and the hairdresser added more red highlights to my hair, which brought out the green in my eyes. I sure looked better, and it lifted my spirits.

For the first time since his leaving, I had a sense of hope. In anticipation of Peter's homecoming. I baked his favorite cookies—chocolate chip. While Noelani and I were shopping, I purchased a darling black nightgown to wear for his return. But the week came and went with no Peter and no word from him. It had been two weeks now since he left for Oahu. I was beginning to wonder if he was ever coming home.

"Hi, Noelani. This is Lyndie. I was curious if you've heard from Peter? He hasn't come home yet." I could hear the concern in her voice. "That's odd. I just assumed he was home and thought I'd give you two time alone. Maybe I should have his dad call him to make sure everything's all right. I'll let you know as soon as Kimo gets in touch with him."

Later that evening Noelani phoned, "Kimo spoke with Peter and he assured his dad that all was well. He told Peter he needed to come home."

"Did he say when he'd be coming back?"

"No, my dear, he didn't. Kimo's upset with him. He thinks he's being irresponsible."

After that I stopped trying to communicate with Peter. I'd grown tired of leaving numerous messages and sending unanswered texts each day. I knew I couldn't force him to come back to me. He'd have to return as long as he wanted to. But what would I do while I waited? I remembered Pastor Stangel mentioned at our wedding reception he could use volunteers. This sounded like a perfect way to keep my mind off Peter.

$\backsim$15$\backsim$

The Betrayal

"Peter will find his way home," Pastor Stangel said one day while I helped at the church. "But first he must find his way to God."

Two more weeks passed. I refused to let fear take over. I knew I must stay strong and trust God would bring my Peter home. Late one night, a knock on the door startled me, and I was surprised to find Kimo waiting on the front porch.

"Is something wrong?" I asked, my heart thumping in my chest.

Kimo shook his head. "No, I just need to talk to you."

"Come into the kitchen, and I'll make some coffee."

"Noelani told me she shared with you about our first year of marriage and how I'd run back to my mom's, but she didn't tell you all of it. I was very immature and selfish and always wanted my own way. The second time I left and went to my mother's house, Noelani came and got me."

"What did she do?"

"She confronted me, saying, 'You have a wife now who loves you, and we are a family. You can't run away every time we have a conflict. We have to work things out together. That's what a husband and wife do.' She showed me the scripture that says a man must leave his mother and father and cleave to his wife. I realized she was right, and I never ran away again."

My heart warmed at his willingness to disclose the details of the story. "Thanks for sharing that."

He nodded. "I know my son loves you with all his heart. I

100

see how he looks at you. He's simply confused now. It's time for you to go get your man."

"Are you sure?"

"Sure enough that I booked a flight for you to Oahu tomorrow afternoon."

Tears filled my eyes as I hugged Kimo. "I do love Peter," I said, "and I want, more than anything else, for us to be happy. You're right. I'll go bring Peter home, then we can be a family again."

On the plane to Oahu, I rehearsed what I'd say to Peter. When the plane landed, I took a taxi to the hotel across the street from Peter's club. I hadn't called him, and I asked his parents not to tell him I was coming. I wanted him to be surprised.

As soon as I checked into my room, I took a shower and put on the pale, yellow pantsuit Noelani had bought for me. After I fixed my hair and redid my makeup, I decided it would be a smart thing to confirm that Peter was at his club before I went there.

"Is Mr. Stanton in?" I asked, disguising my voice.

"No, I'm sorry. He isn't due back until five. Is there a message?"

"No, I'll phone him back. Thank you very much."

Hungry and feeling impatient, I went downstairs to the coffee shop to get a bite to eat. I sat outside at a table on the patio, but the longer I sat, the more nervous I became. What if Peter gets angry with me for showing up? What if he tells me to go home?

A black BMW pulled up to the curb, interrupting my thoughts. Peter got out of the front passenger seat, then went around to open the driver side door. An extremely attractive blonde nearly fell out of the car and into his arms. Peter kissed her long and hard, the way he'd once kissed me. From my chair I could hear their exchange.

"I'll come back to the club to get you at eleven," the blonde cooed. "I'll miss you until then."

"I'll miss you too, Jeannie," Peter answered, then kissed her again.

I stood to leave. Trembling, I held onto my chair for a moment, not believing my husband was kissing another woman.

"Are you all right? You look as if you've seen a ghost." The server asked.

Worse than that, I thought, and handed her a $20 bill.

She scurried after me. "Your change, miss."

"Keep it."

I hurried up to my room and fell on the bed. I felt like the wind had been knocked out of me. I shook. I wanted to leave and go home, but I couldn't. Home was where Peter and I were supposed to live together—not me there and him here with another woman.

I threw my things into the suitcase, and within minutes I was in a taxi.

"Where to, miss?"

"Take me to the airport, Hawaiian Air."

I decided I didn't care what the cost of a last-minute flight was. I just needed to get away. When I arrived at the ticket counter, I found I'd just missed a plane to Kauai. The next one wasn't scheduled to leave for nearly two hours. I slumped into a chair and tried not to cry as I waited for my flight.

Once onboard I took a window seat and looked out, wondering if I should have confronted Peter and that woman. What was her name again? I can't remember. But why does it matter? I would have made a fool of myself if I'd confronted them.

The plane landed just before nine. The thought of seeing my in-laws too unbearable, I spent the night at the Holiday Inn by the airport. I needed to think and figure out what I should do. I wanted to call Pastor Stangel and Karen, but I knew it was probably too late.

Exhausted and scared the marriage I'd always wanted was over for good, I prayed, "Please God help me. I don't know what to do." I cried myself to sleep.

⌒16⌒

Yielded

The sun coming in through the window woke me. At first, I thought I'd imagined the whole thing. Everything I'd seen the day before was a horrible nightmare. But it was real. I saw Peter with another woman. I knew I couldn't hide out in the hotel forever. It was time to face Peter's parents.

After I grabbed a coffee and bagel from the hotel restaurant, I sat in the lobby eating while I waited for the taxi. In minutes I was in the backseat, heading for my in-law's place. The cab driver was a cheery Hawaiian man, but his cheerful tone just loosed the tears to cascade down my face.

"Is everything okay, young lady?"

"I'm fine," I lied.

He cleared his throat. "I can't fix things," he said, "but I can introduce you to someone who can." He pointed to a cross hanging from the mirror. "Jesus said, 'Cast all your cares on me because I care for you.'"

"I've heard that before."

"From someone who cared greatly about you, I figure." He glanced at me in the mirror again.

That's right. I heard it from dear sweet Sam. How I longed to speak to him at that moment. I knew he'd help me work things out. But Sam was far away, and—

I glanced out the window in time to see us whizzing past Pastor Stangel's church. The sign out front grabbed my attention. "Only one person loved you enough to die for you."

"Stop the cab!"

The driver slammed on the brakes.

"Please drive back to that church."

"Sure, miss. That's my church." We pulled up to the front, and I re-read the sign—this time out loud.

The driver said, "That's talking about John 3:16, among other scriptures. Jesus loves us so much. Do you know him?"

"I thought I did."

A car pulled up next to us then. "Keoni, is there a problem with your cab?"

"No, Pastor. This young lady wanted to read your sign."

I sucked in a deep breath. "Pastor Stangel, I'm so happy you're here."

His kindness melted my façade. "Hello, Lyndie. How are you doing? Can I help you with something?"

I broke into sobs, though I'd tried in vain to hold them back.

"Would you like to come in for a minute and talk with me and my wife?"

I glanced at the cab driver, not knowing what to say.

"I'll go get us some coffee and stop back to check if you still need a ride," he said.

I followed Pastor Stangel into the church, a humble little building with magnificent stained-glass windows. I'd felt a presence of peace each time I stepped into this building. Pastor took me into his office to the right of the sanctuary. "Have a seat in here, and I'll be back in a few minutes with Karen."

"Let's have a word of prayer," Pastor Stangel suggested, moments after they returned. We bowed out heads. "Dear Lord Jesus," he prayed, "I believe You've sent Lyndie here. I know You love her unconditionally. If she'd been the only person on this earth, You'd have died just for her. I ask You now to heal her from the wounds of the past. Let her know she doesn't have to hurt anymore. You took all her pain on the cross at Calvary. In Jesus' name, amen."

After the prayer I wept and poured out my heart. I told them everything that had transpired in my life from the day I went shopping with my mother as a young girl to what happened the day before in Oahu. I included the disgusting details from my past, things I thought I'd never be able to share with anyone. And I told them all about my hero, Sam, how that wonderful man had saved my life and introduced me to Jesus.

They listened patiently during my nearly thirty-minute ramble. When I was finished, I felt as if a massive weight had been lifted from my shoulders.

The pastor took my hand. "Sam introduced you to Jesus, and you accepted him as Savior, but you allowed shame, fear, guilt, and condemnation to come into your heart. You need to make Jesus the Lord of your life. You do that by getting into His Word—the Bible—and trusting what it says." He looked at Karen who took my other hand.

"Then you'll be able to use the scriptures to fight the enemy when feelings of unworthiness creep in," she explained. "The Bible says the Word of God is sharper than any two-edged sword."

A knock on the door interrupted us at that moment. "Come in," Karen invited Keoni, the taxi driver.

"So sorry to interrupt," he said, "but I just wanted to see if the little lady needs me to take her home."

"Thanks, Keoni," the pastor answered. "We'll take care of it."

The cab driver nodded humbly. "All right. I'll bring her luggage and set it in the church."

"I really appreciate your kindness. Thank you, Keoni," I said.

"I'll be praying for you, sister," he said, as he turned and walked away.

Pastor Stangel opened the Bible to the book of Ephesians and explained about putting on the whole armor of God. "Also, Lyndie, in Psalms, it says, 'The Lord is near to the broken-hearted and saves the crushed in spirit.' Your heart is broken now, and your spirit is crushed, but Jesus can mend them."

Karen handed me a tissue as tears trickled down my cheeks.

"What Peter is doing to you right now isn't right," pastor continued. "But Peter's reacting in his flesh. You've hurt him and his ego since you haven't totally given yourself to him in this marriage. He's obviously looking to find satisfaction elsewhere. You can't go into a marriage without the truth. You should have told him the truth from the beginning. A marriage is between three people—God, the man, and the woman."

I leaned forward in my chair. "I remember when you had us braid 'God's knot,' the three-fold cord, at our wedding. You talked about how the man and wife need to stay connected to God for their marriage to work out."

He nodded. "Ecclesiastics says, 'Though one may be overpowered, two can defend themselves. A cord of three strands is not easily broken.'" He paused for a moment. "I think you and Peter took part in this ceremony, but you two never really gave your whole heart to the Lord. Jesus needs to be the Lord over your entire life. If God is truly invited into a marriage, He works right alongside you. You and Peter needed to be praying every day and trusting God. The good news is that it's never too late. The Bible says, 'Nothing is impossible with God.' What you've told me about Peter proves to me that he loves you dearly. He's hurt now, and in his time of weakness, the enemy brought this woman into his life to put a bandage on his hurt. He's running away from you, himself, and mostly God. I've known Peter since he was a little boy, and he's been running away for a long time. He knows he's wrong."

"So, what do I do?"

"Pray and trust God. After all, God loves Peter more than you ever could. Start reading your Bible, come to church, and allow God to heal you. Peter will come around. Do you still have the Bible Sam gave you?"

I nodded. "Yes, I still have it."

"You're going to have to lean on God's strength because, in

the next couple of months, you're going to have to deal with the truth and face those you love and who love you. I think you need to start with Peter's parents. If you'd like I could have them come here, and I'll briefly share your story, leaving out some of the horrid details."

"You'd do that? It would be too painful for me to tell them."

"I think you need compassionate, supportive people close to you now. I know Kimo and Noelani personally and well. They used to be members of this church. Then when Peter's younger sister was killed in an auto accident, they stopped coming."

I was stunned. "I didn't even know they had a daughter."

"We reached out to them, but they were angry with God and blamed him for what happened to their child. You're an answer to prayer. It sounds as though they love you like a daughter. You've brought joy back into their lives. Maybe now that they recognize the need for you to be in church, you can all come as a family."

I was still trying to digest the news that Peter had once had a sister. "Peter and his parents have never mentioned her."

"Her name was Leimomi, a lovely girl." He smiled. "I think this is the time for truth and healing." He excused himself to go contact Peter's parents.

Karen took my hand. "Would you like to pray?"

I nodded, slipped from the chair, and dropped to my knees. Karen joined me, her hand on my shoulder. "Jesus, please help me. Help me to lay down at Your feet all the dreadful memories of what I was forced to do. Let me realize it wasn't my fault. Please erase those memories and replace them with loving, wholesome ones. Help Peter to let go of his hurts too. Bring him home to me, Lord. Let me love him like a woman should love a man. Bless Sam, and keep him and Sandy well. Bless my parents and Tommy. Help them to understand and forgive me."

We'd just reseated ourselves when the pastor returned with the news that Peter's parents were on their way. "I told them you were here with me. They were grateful to hear you're safe. I also explained that it was necessary for me to talk with them before they take you home."

While we waited for their arrival, we prayed Kimo and Noelani would be sensitive to all Pastor Stangel would share with them.

≈17≈

Trusting and Healing

While we waited for my in-laws to arrive, Karen took me into the kitchen to fix me some brunch. I sipped coffee while she made scrambled eggs and toast.

A picture of Jesus hung on the wall. His eyes seemed to bore right into my soul, and a sense of peace overcame me, a knowing that everything would work out fine.

After a while Pastor Stangel strode into the kitchen smiling. "Kimo and Noelani are ready to take you home. They want to come back on Sunday and bring you to church with them. They love you like a daughter, and they promised to be by your side throughout all of this."

I felt as if a heavy load had been lifted off my back. "Thanks for doing this for me."

He patted my shoulder. "They understand what you've been through and why you feel like you can't contact your parents, and they want to help you reconcile with them. They confirmed that Peter loves you, and they know he'll do the right thing and come home. They'll agree in prayer with you for that."

I hugged Pastor Stangel, then together we walked out into the hallway. Peter's parents were waiting; both were crying.

"Oh, Lyndie," Noelani sobbed, "we love you. You are family now, and we're dreadfully sorry for what you've endured." They put their arms around me, and we waved good-bye to Pastor Stangel and Karen.

In the privacy of the car, tears glistened once more on Kimo's cheeks. "We're immensely grateful for you, Lyndie. You opened our eyes. The Stangel's are wonderful, loving people of

God. We should have listened to them a long time ago and not strayed away from the church. In our hearts we knew God didn't cause the accident that took our Leimomi's life, but it was easier to blame God than to accept our hurt."

During the drive to their home, Noelani confessed she was relieved she could now speak openly about her daughter. "We would like for you to have dinner with us."

"Thanks for the offer. I don't know if I'm quite ready to return home."

After dinner Noelani brought out an album with pictures of Leimomi. With tears in her eyes, she showed me the photos, assuring me her tears were no longer tears of sadness but of joy.

Leimomi was a beautiful girl with dark round eyes and striking long black hair. Peter was in many of the photographs with his sister. Photos of him teaching her to surf and to ride a horse tugged at my heart, as did pictures of them goofing around, the way siblings do. Kimo and Noelani had also taken lots of pictures of Leimomi dancing the hula. I felt extremely blessed to be a part of this family's healing.

The following day we attended church together. The worship team sang a beautiful song proclaiming God's love for us. Pastor Stangel's sermon captured my attention. "Hebrews 13:5 tells us God will never leave us nor forsake us. We may walk away from God, but He never walks away from us. And even when we do, He is always waiting with open arms for us to return."

At the end of the service, during the invitation to come to the altar for prayer, Peter's parents and I went forward and recommitted our lives to Christ. I felt free, as if I'd at last laid down a heavy burden.

Pastor Stangel greeted us at the door as we left. "Just keep praying and trust God to take care of Peter. Keep believing that Peter will find his way home."

Every morning for the next few weeks, I awakened early

and dropped to my knees in prayer. I started by thanking God for delivering me from my kidnappers. I thanked him for Kimo and Noelani and asked him to bless them. Next, I prayed for my parents, Tommy, Sam, and of course, Peter. Then I read the Bible Sam had given me.

When I read it, I felt like I was reading a love letter God had written just for me. I stopped thinking about myself and started getting to know Jesus. Little by little my shame and hurt disappeared. God even brought me to a place where I could forgive those who sold me, abused me, and held me in bondage. At some point I began to pray they would come to know Jesus. I put Philippians 4:7 up on the mirror in my bathroom where I could see it often: "And the peace of God, which transcends all understanding, will guard your hearts and your minds in Christ Jesus." It brought comfort to my heart every time I read it.

I didn't contact Peter, nor did he contact me. I struggled with the decision not to contact him, but I had to believe God was in control. I did learn from Noelani and Kimo that Peter had phoned them a couple times. Each time they talked, they asked him when he was coming home. He told them when he finished his business there. They didn't press him further, but they decided they'd meet with me once a week to pray for my marriage and to study the Bible.

We began our study in the Gospel of John. I learned it was written so those who read it would believe in Jesus and have a new life. The Gospel of John depicts Jesus' preexistent life with the Father, showing Jesus was not simply a great man but also God. Jesus is described as love, light, truth, the good Shepherd, the door, the resurrection, and the life, living water, and the bread of life. John not only stresses the deity of Jesus but provides an interpretation of His life. The Gospel of John displays God's great love for believers, which is why it is often called "the love gospel."

One night after studying the Word, Kimo mentioned when

Peter and Leimomi were young, people gathered in their home weekly for fellowship and Bible study. That gave me an idea. "Why don't you ask Pastor Stangel if you can do a home group again?"

Kimo's face lit up. "That's a great idea. We'll do that when Peter comes home."

Noelani and Kimo always encouraged me, reminding me not to lose hope and to trust God.

"Just like God brought us back," Kimo said, "keep believing he'll turn Peter's heart back to him and direct his steps home to you."

One morning I woke early and went into the bathroom to wash, but the water coming out of the faucet was rust colored. When I went to look outside, there were wet patches around the back of the house, and I could hear a hissing sound. That's it, I thought. I'm calling Kimo.

Kimo checked the faucets first. "There's quite a change in the water pressure. Have your water bills gone up lately?"

"Well, now that you mention it, they have increased considerably in the last two months."

He nodded, "I think you have an underground water leak. This is beyond what I can fix. Let's look for a plumber."

I booked a plumber to come in the afternoon.

"Call me if you need anything," Kimo said as he was leaving.

Opening my Bible to the book of Ruth, I read there's no such thing as an unimportant person in God's eyes. Few people saw Ruth as important, but God saw her as an important part in the lineage of Jesus. She was the grandmother of King David.

"Lord," I prayed, "I want to be part of Your plan."

I busied myself cleaning the house until the plumber arrived. "Hey, I'm Keomi. I'll check the inside water pressure and plumbing inside the house first, then I'll see what's going on outside."

"Okay, thanks for coming," Following him outside, as he bent over I noticed his broad tan shoulders. He turned around and smiled at me. I took a step back and my face grew hot. *Oh, no, Lord, I don't need to give this guy any ideas.* It was too late. Keomi moved in too close, and I was immediately enveloped by his sweat mixed with cologne. My head was spinning as he endeavored to explain the problem and repair cost.

"Mrs. Stanton, where's your husband?" he asked, his voice nearly crooning. "You're a beautiful woman. It must get lonely in the house all alone. I know I could make you feel good."

Shocked, I ran into the house, locking the door behind me. The laughing and mocking began in my head. *You have a scent that men pick up on—they all know what kind of woman you are.*

Trembling, I picked up the phone and called my in-laws. "Kimo, please come over. The plumber is here, and I want to make sure he's not cheating me."

Kimo came right over and stayed until Keomi fixed the leak. I gave Kimo the check to pay the plumber and said, "I need some fresh air. I'm going for a walk on the beach."

Walking along the shore and looking at the immensity of the water in the Pacific Ocean, I wished I could just wash all the filth of my past away. I don't want to be a sex object. I lamented silently. Then words from the Bible quietly spoke into my heart: "I will cleanse you as white as snow."

Encouraged, I walked slowly back to the house.

As my faith in Jesus grew, I rested in him, knowing He'd bring Peter back to me. I was so sure of this. I began to prepare myself and our home for Peter's imminent return.

I spent many hours with Lehua Prasser, a Christian counselor who specialized in helping women who'd been sexually abused, as she walked me through the inner healing process and prayed with me. She also taught me what the Bible says about being a loving wife. I wanted to be able to accept, enjoy, and respond to the intimacy Peter and I deserved in our marriage.

In addition to seeing a counselor, I spent time decorating our home with things I knew would please my husband. I planted an organic vegetable garden and more fruit trees in our backyard. I also put myself on an exercise and running regimen, enabling me to be in excellent physical shape.

Three months had passed since I had caught Peter with the blonde woman. Every time the enemy bombarded my mind with negative thoughts, I refused to entertain them. Instead, I replaced them with the Word and the promises of God.

⁓18⁓

Reunited

One particularly beautiful morning after my quiet time praying and reading my Bible, I took a quick shower and saddled my horse for a ride along the beach, leaving a quick message with my in-laws about my plans. Riding along the shore, I witnessed the most magnificent sunrise. Soaking in God's amazing creation, I thanked him and started singing a song I'd learned at church about loving God in the morning when you see the sun rising. I stopped mid-song and halted my horse as I noticed a figure walking down the beach toward me. I squinted.

"Oh, Lord!" I whispered. Could it be? Yes. Yes, it was! "Thank You, Lord!"

I jumped off my horse and ran straight to him. We collided into each other's arms.

"Peter!" I cried. "My husband!"

"Oh, Lyndie, Lyndie! Please, forgive me. I've been such a fool. I love you with my whole being. You're the best thing that ever happened to me, and I couldn't bear to lose you. I swear, I'll never leave you again."

"Oh, Peter," I laughed, hanging on as he spun me around, "I love you too. I'm sorry too. Forgive me for not telling you the truth and for denying you the rights of a husband. I've been praying and believing God would bring you home."

"And that He did," Peter answered, setting me back down. "I went to our house first, but when I didn't find you there, I went to my parents' house. That's how I knew you were riding on the beach. Wait until I tell you my story of what God has done in my life. Mom and Dad shared you all have gone back to

Kapaa Christian Fellowship with Pastor Stangel. Honey, I want to go to church too. I know if we truly invite God into our home, we can survive anything. He's the one who can restore and strengthen our marriage."

"And I'll never give you a reason to leave again," I promised. "I'll never, ever let you leave."

Hand-in-hand, we walked toward our house.

"What did you mean by your story?" I asked, hoping I wasn't going to hear anything about his relationship with that other woman.

He grinned down at me. "It's amazing. Wait until you hear what happened to me! I haven't even told my parents yet. I want you all to be together to hear what God did."

We returned the horse to the barn and headed over to Noelani and Kimo's house. When we strolled, yet again hand-in-hand, through their front door, they hugged us and clapped and shouted. "We told you God would bring him home," Kimo hugged me. "But first we all need to thank God for this great miracle."

The four of us held hands and prayed together. Before Peter began his story, he pulled me aside. "Lyndie, when I came looking for you today, my parents told me you saw me with that woman. Oh, sweetheart, I'm so sorry! Please forgive me. She didn't mean anything to me, I promise you. She was just a diversion the enemy brought into my life to distract me from the woman I love. I don't want the things I'm about to share with all of you to hurt you anymore than you've already been hurt."

I placed my hands on his cheeks as I gazed up into his eyes. "It's all right. I forgive you, Peter. I realize the enemy put her in your path to steer you away from God and take you from me."

Noelani called us then. "I'm going to get us some cold drinks. Why don't we all go sit out on the lanai? It's such a beautiful day."

Comfortably situated on the couches with drinks and

snacks, Peter plunged into his story. "Late one night a few days ago, I was at Jeannie's house. She wouldn't stop pushing me to get a divorce, and we'd been drinking heavily. When I told her I didn't want to do that, she started screaming and throwing things at me. She warned me that if I didn't comply with her wishes, she'd let my wife know what I'd been doing." He paused, a slight flush mounting on his cheeks. "I stormed out of her house with a bottle of alcohol. I drove to the North Shore, drinking the whole way. The last thing I remember is pulling over to throw up. I must have been really drunk and passed out."

My hand flew up to my cheek. "Oh, my love, you could have been in an accident. I know my prayers protected you."

He nodded. "I know it too. I woke up with the sun blazing in my face. I looked around through bloodshot eyes and found myself in the parking lot of a church. I was about six inches from the sign in front that said, 'Don't run away from God. He is the only one who can fix all your mistakes.' A few minutes later, a guy pulled up right behind my car."

Peter paused again and looked at each of us for a moment. "I thought he was a cop, about to reprimand me for ruining the flower bed, which I'd apparently driven through hours earlier. Instead, he asked, 'Are you all right, son?'"

One look at the empty bottle of alcohol on the floor, combined with me smelling like vomit, gave him his answer. He introduced himself as Pastor Art, then said to follow him into the church where he could make me some strong coffee. We went into the church kitchen, where he not only brewed the coffee but also cooked us both some bacon, eggs, and toast."

I glanced at Peter's mom, who sat with a hand over her mouth. His father was expressionless, his hands resting in his lap.

"While we were eating," Peter continued, "he assured me God had spared my life. He told me God had a reason for bringing me there. It was no accident I almost crashed into the church. Next, he reminded me of how much God loves me. I just broke down and began recounting my entire life story from the time Leimomi was killed in the car accident to leaving Lyndie and becoming involved with this woman on Oahu. I shared with him my family and I had been in church, but we were angry with God ever since my sister's senseless death. I disclosed the problem we were having in our marriage, Lyndie, but I also told him that I truly loved my wife with my whole heart."

I smiled at Peter and put my hand on his.

"After that, Pastor Art walked me into the chapel and prayed with me. I confessed my sins and asked Jesus for forgiveness. Then the pastor counseled me to go home and let God heal my marriage." He smiled at me and continued. "I went back to Waikiki, showered, packed, and got on the first plane to Kauai. And here I am."

Kimo blinked back tears as he said, "Now let Lyndie tell you her story. It's remarkably similar to yours."

I told of my adventure to Oahu to confront him, what happened on the way home from the airport, and how the message on the church stopped me. I also told him how Pastor Stangel pulled up at the exact moment I was reading the sign.

Peter took my hand in his. "God must really want us together. You're my family, Lyndie, and I love you with all my heart."

"Yes, she is family," Kimo said. "God brought her, not only to you, but for us too. He used Lyndie to bring healing to this family."

Peter leaned over and kissed me, and a sense of desire shot through me like I'd never known before. I was sure it showed on my face.

Noelani giggled. "I think it's time for you two to be heading home."

I blushed as Peter pulled me up from the couch. On the way

to the ranch house, neither of us spoke, but I rested my head on Peter's shoulder the entire way.

Peter's eyes lit up when he saw what I'd done with the house. He walked through each room and stopped in the kitchen. "Lyndie, you've done a fabulous job of making our house into a home. I love everything you did ..." He paused and put his hands on my arms. "And I love you." He pulled me into a big hug, then kissed my lips, slow and easy, while brushing back a wisp of my hair.

I let go of the embrace and turned toward the bedroom. "I'm going to take a bath. Why don't you open a bottle of champagne? I've kept it cold in the refrigerator to celebrate your homecoming."

His smile was as warm as my heart felt. "Sounds like a plan, honey. But first I'm going to use the other bathroom and take a quick shower."

As I sat soaking in the tub, I realized I longed for Peter in a vastly different way. With my desire growing I dressed in a blue satin negligee I'd purchased by faith to celebrate when Peter returned. Glancing at myself in the mirror, I was pleased with what I saw. My healthy diet and exercise had paid off. I felt—and looked—alluring. Quietly I snuck into the living room.

Peter had his back to me. The champagne glasses sat on the cocktail table, filled and ready for us to drink. I snuck up behind him and put my arms around his waist, then stood on my toes and passionately kissed him on the neck.

He turned, paused, and with eyes open wide in obvious delight, said, "Look at my adorable wife. I sure have missed you, baby."

We cuddled on the couch and drank a glass of champagne. Then he lifted me and carried me into our bedroom. What happened next was incredible. With all my reserves gone, I melted into Peter and was finally able to give my whole self to him.

The next morning, as I laid enveloped in Peter's loving

arms, I thanked God. "Thank You, Father, for bringing Peter home to me and for allowing me to respond to him as his wife."

≈19≈

Truth

Two days after Peter's return, I couldn't get out of bed. My head pounded, and my body wouldn't move, paralyzed with fear as a nagging question plagued me: *What if Peter gets tired of me and cheats again? Do I just perform for him out of fear that I don't measure up to the woman he had the affair with?* Guilt and shame gripped me.

This can't be the way a Christian marriage should be, I thought. A marriage needs trust, not fear. But trust requires truth. I blamed myself for Peter's infidelity. I should have told him the truth from the beginning. I'm guilty of deception. I'm sexually broken. We need help. I must tell Peter everything.

I walked out into the kitchen where Peter was making coffee. He looked amazingly handsome and happy, and I was about spoil his mood. But I'd made the decision, and I couldn't let myself back off now.

"We need to talk. Please sit down."

He frowned. "Honey, what's wrong? You look upset."

I took a deep breath. "I assume your parents shared with you about my years in captivity. But I need to tell you everything, something I should have done a long time ago."

Peter and I sat down at the table. Hot tears burned my eyes, and my chest tightened, but I plowed ahead, divulging my entire story.

Peter moved in closer and took my hand. Tears dripped down his cheeks as my story unfolded. When I finished, he held me close, rocking back and forth.

"Oh, sweetheart, I'm really sorry. If I'd only known all this sooner, we could have gotten help together. I've only added to your pain by my behavior."

"Peter, after everything those men did to me," I said, swiping at my tears, "I never thought I could ever trust a man. Then I met you. I trusted you, and you let me down. Now I have this fear I could do something to make you cheat on me again."

"But I never would."

I nodded. "I know you mean that, but I think we need counseling to rebuild trust in our relationship."

"I'm going to phone Pastor Stangel right now." When he hung up, he gave me a hopeful look. "He can meet us this afternoon."

We arrived at the church. Pastor Stangel took my arm. "Karen is waiting for us here in my office. You folks sit down on the couch and make yourselves comfortable." I was a bit hesitant at first to share my true thoughts and feelings, but eventually I was able to share my fear and the blame I felt for Peter having an affair.

My confession ended as a single sob slipped from my throat. "When Peter came home, I just wanted him to grab me, hold me, love me, and make everything go away. But in my mind, I kept seeing him with that woman."

I saw the agony on Peter's face as he spoke, his voice barely above a whisper. "I see the pain I caused Lyndie. What I did was thoughtless and cruel. In my own selfish ego, I felt justified. I wanted to hurt her for not fulfilling me as a man. Lust came into my heart. I allowed myself to be seduced by this woman. My desire for sex blinded me to the genuine love of my wife."

Pastor Stangel nodded. "Before I became a pastor, my wife and I were licensed counselors. We've seen the pain infidelity causes. Both of you need to better understand the redemptive love of God. Peter, I'd like for you to start attending an ongoing faith-based program called Hope Restored, sponsored by Focus on the Family. A new session starts in Lihue next week. Several pastors and I will be there to assist with discipleship."

He paused and looked at both of us.

"In the program you'll be assigned a mentor to pray with and be accountable to. During these sessions you'll be studying Dr. Doug Weiss's DVD series 'Helping Her Heal.' This series will help you understand the weight of Lyndie's pain and learn to validate that pain."

Peter nodded. "Whatever it takes. I want to help my wife."

Karen looked and me. "While Peter's attending these meetings, I'd like you to come here, and together we can do a study on shame. There's a wonderful DVD series by Christine Caine entitled 'Unashamed' and a book study by Heather Nelson with the same title. I believe it'll help in your healing process. You've been damaged and broken." She took my hand. "Now that the truth is out, we need to reorganize your life around the One who is truth."

The four of us shared a final prayer, and we headed home. In the comfort of our living room, Peter took my head in his hands and looked into my eyes. "I'm going to put all I have into this marriage and helping you to heal."

My chin trembled, and tears rolled down my cheeks. In my heart I knew his reason for saying that came from a devotion deeper than anything anyone had ever felt for me. He loves and cares for me. We can make this work.

For the next several weeks, Peter rushed home from the program, eager to share what he'd learned in the meeting. I saw the changes in my husband, and I knew the program was working. Peter was more sensitive to my needs and even offered to help me around the house. I was delighted the day he said to me, "I'm learning how to renew my mind."

"And I'm learning that when I feel rejected, I need to remember who God says I am," I said as I snuggled into his embrace.

The more I saw Peter trying to understand my pain, the closer to him I felt.

⪦20⪧

It's Time

Peter and I attended Kapaa Community Church regularly. His parents hosted a weekly Bible study in their home, Peter continued his counseling program, and I went to weekly Bible studies with Karen. Six months after Peter's return home, the Stangels invited us to their office. After asking us how things were going at home, Pastor Stangel announced, "It's time."

"Time for what?" I asked.

With his eyes fixed on me, the pastor said, "Peter's been home for some time now, God is healing your marriage, and you're growing in your faith and serving him. God is restoring you from your past."

He turned to Peter. "It's time for you to take your wife to see her family and Sam. They deserve to know their daughter is alive and to know the truth of what happened over all those years. Now that she's recovering from her past, she needs a relationship with her parents. I'm sure they'd want to be part of her life now. And she owes it to Sam to explain what happened to the seed he planted in her life."

Surprisingly, instead of being fearful I felt excited. Pastor Stangel suggested we communicate with Sam and my parents before we arrive. He believed this would not only lessen the shock for them but also give them time to prepare.

As usual Peter made all the arrangements, scheduling us to leave in two and a half months, so he could finish the eight months of his counseling program. We would arrive on the mainland July first and be gone for two weeks.

Peter booked us into Salt Lake City to see Sam first. We

also invited him to come with us to visit my parents. I knew I'd be braver with Sam there. Peter offered to pay for his ticket, and Sam thanked Peter for his generosity but declined the offer. However, he said he'd be honored to accompany us. We would visit Sam, then fly into Dulles International Airport, the closest airport to my parents' home in Maryland.

Six weeks before we were to leave, I woke up feeling awful. I began vomiting, my head hurt, and I was dizzy. Peter immediately insisted I go see a doctor. Noelani offered to drive me to my appointment, since Peter was helping Kimo replace the roof on his father's house.

On the way to the doctor's office, Noelani said, "I'm thrilled you and Peter are going to see your folks. I can't wait to meet them all and tell them how grateful I am to have you as my daughter-in-law."

I felt my eyes brighten as I smiled.

The doctor's waiting room was packed. A salt-water aquarium covered one wall. The chairs were close together, and I couldn't help but notice one woman wore the most awful smelling perfume. We settled in for a long, unpleasant wait. I still felt nauseated and dizzy, and my stomach hurt. Maybe I have the flu. I ran into the restroom to throw up several times as we waited.

Finally, the nurse called my name. Doctor Klein, a tall, Norwegian-looking man who seemed out of place on Kauai, hurried in. "So young lady, I've done a thorough exam but I'm wondering—might you be pregnant?

"Pregnant?" My heart quickened, and I clutched my hands together, trying to steady my trembling. Did I dare hope?

I impatiently waited for the results for what seemed like hours. Doctor Klein returned. "Well, young lady, congratulations. You're going to be a mother."

"Oh, I'm going to be a mother!" The words popped out before I could even think about what I was saying, and then it seemed my brain shut down and I couldn't think of another thing to say. My hand flew to my mouth, and I started giggling as a feeling of absolute joy swept over me and brought tears to my eyes.

"I've scheduled an ultrasound for you in four weeks," the doctor said. "You'll be eighteen weeks along by then, and we'll be able to discern the baby's sex. I'm sure you folks want to know if you're having a boy or a girl."

Weak-kneed, I returned to the waiting area, giggling at Noelani's inquisitive look.

She stood to her feet. "Well, what did the doctor say was wrong with you?"

"Wrong?" I couldn't stop myself from smiling. "Nothing's wrong. In fact, I couldn't be better."

Noelani's eyes widened. "Oh, my! You're pregnant, aren't you?" she shouted, drawing the attention of everyone else in the room.

Before Noelani could air more of our personal business, I hustled her out of the office. But she chattered excitedly all the way to the car.

"Peter's going to be a father, and I'm going to be a grand-mother!" Her face shone. "Wait 'til he and Kimo hear the news!"

All the way home, I could scarcely sit still, and both of us chatted incessantly. "Not only is God healing and restoring me," I declared, "reconciling our marriage, allowing me to reconnect with my family and Sam, but now he's giving me a child too."

We no sooner pulled into their driveway, my husband climbed down from the roof and came to hug me. "What was Dr. Klein's prognosis? Is everything okay?"

Noelani and I grinned and winked at one another, as Peter grew more visibly anxious.

"Well, what did he say?" he demanded.

"Peter, we're going to have a baby!"

"You've made me the happiest man in the world," he declared, as he twirled me around.

"Hey, you be gentle with her now," Noelani wagged a finger at her son.

Peter smiled sheepishly. "Yes, Mom. Well, is it a boy or a girl?"

"We'll know when I go in for an ultrasound in four weeks."

Kimo came out of the house then, carrying two water bottles. "Hey, what's all the excitement about?"

"I'm having a baby," Peter announced, then chuckled. "Well, Lyndie's having a baby."

Kimo's face lit up as he pulled us into a bear hug. "That's wonderful! I'm full of happiness for you both—for all of us. And what great news to bring to your parents and Sam."

Peter nodded. "Yes, Dad. God has truly given us a great gift to share with Lyndie's family."

I should have been excited. I was about to find out the sex of my child. I simply couldn't shake the horrible thought I didn't deserve good things.

I kept seeing the faces of Hank and all the men who'd abused me. They laughed at me and shouted, "What kind of a mother would you make?" My ribcage throbbed as the scenarios flooded my mind and tears soaked my pillow.

Peter entered the bedroom and hurried to sit down on the edge of the bed. "What's wrong, sweetheart? Is the baby all right?" He wrapped his arms around me and pulled me against his chest, launching a fresh onslaught of tears, quickly soaking his shirt.

"I feel so unworthy to enjoy the happiness of our child and I can't get the awful images of my captivity out of my mind," I managed to choke out.

He pulled back to look into my face, wiping tears from my hot cheeks with his finger. His face filled with compassion. "No. All of that is a lie. You are worthy because of your new life in Christ."

I knew he was right, and I was so grateful when he led us in prayer. It wasn't long until I fell asleep in his arms.

———•———

Peter was more excited and anxious about the ultrasound than I was.

"Sit down, Peter. You're a bundle of nerves." Dr. Klein laughed.

"Yes sir."

"Well, look at that!" Dr. Klein said not long after beginning the procedure. "Looks like you need to start shopping for some hair bows, Peter."

"A girl!" Peter yelled, jumping up from his seat. "We're having a little girl!"

From that moment forward, Peter treated me like a delicate princess. "I'm not going to let you do any housework or lift anything heavy. We can hire one of auntie's friends to clean our house. No more horseback riding either. Before the ultrasound, the doctor warned me about the motion of jostling while on a horse. He explained it could increase the risk of placental absorption—a pregnancy complication that occurs when the placenta detaches from the uterus too early."

I was impressed with his newfound knowledge about pregnancy but disappointed at the idea of giving up riding, though I knew we needed to keep our baby safe. We even checked with the doctor about our scheduled trip, and Dr. Klein confirmed it was safe for me to fly, but he also cautioned us the importance for me to get plenty of rest while we were gone.

On the drive home, Peter took Dr. Klein's advice and stopped at a children's store, where he bought all the bows they had, as well as a ruffled pink dress. "We'll need to talk about a name for our daughter."

I nodded. "I thought about that last night, before we knew for sure whether we were having a boy or a girl. I decided I'd like to name a boy Sam. But since we're having a girl, how about naming her Samantha Leimomi Stanton?"

"Oh, honey, what a terrific name!" Peter kissed my hand. "My parents will be honored that we chose to carry on their daughter's name."

"What say we stop and tell your parents? I can't wait to share the news with them," I gushed.

Before we'd had a chance to greet each other, Peter burst out with our news. "Mom, Dad, Lyndie's having a girl, and we chose Leimoni as her middle name."

Noelani blinked fresh tears away. "I'm so happy," she said. "I love you both with all my heart."

Kimo grinned from ear to ear. "You've made us incredibly happy today. And we've decided we'd like to buy your nursery furniture. Go to a baby store with Noelani," he told me, "and get anything you need."

I threw my arms around them. "I'm so grateful for your generosity, but more than that, I'm grateful for the two of you. Your support has made me a stronger person. You'll be such a blessing to our little Samantha Leimoni."

Laughing and crying at the same time, we eventually managed to settle down. "What theme did you chose for the nursery?"

I blinked. "Theme?"

"You know— like Winnie the Pooh, Disney Princess, Hello Kitty?"

"Oh, I never thought about that."

"How about we paint the walls a pale pink?" Peter asked. "We can get white nursery furniture and have a Noah's Ark theme. Mom's a super artist. She could paint a mural of the ark and animals on one wall."

"That sounds perfect," I said, planting a kiss on my husband's cheek. "I love your idea."

The night before our trip to the mainland, I fell asleep, excited and happy about the news of a daughter. But soon after I dozed off, my excitement turned into a nightmare. I was running, carrying our baby while Hank chased me with a gun, yelling, "Give me the baby. You're not worthy."

"Leave me alone," I shouted. "Leave me alone!"

In the distance I heard Peter's voice. "Lyndie, wake up. I'm here. No one's going to hurt you. It's only a dream."

≈21≈

Sam

Peter awakened at the crack of dawn to make sure we had everything we needed before leaving for the mainland.

We headed for Lihue Airport with Kimo and Noelani as the sun was rising. We had close to three hours until our Hawaiian Air departure for Honolulu. We chatted about baby things all the way to the airport. While Kimo parked the car and Peter checked our bags, Noelani ran off, leaving me sitting alone in the terminal, wondering where she'd gone.

Kimo and Peter returned at the same time as Noelani, her arms full of leis. Arranging a pikai lei around my neck, Noelani whispered, "I know how much you adore the fragrance of this Arabian jasmine flower." She placed a maile leaf lei on Peter, "These flowers are supposed to last the longest." She handed me a box with three tuberrose leis.

"These are for Sam, your mother, and your father. When you get to Sam's, wrap them in a damp towel and keep them in the bottom of the refrigerator." She reminded me.

"Thank you for your thoughtfulness," I said. "They really are beautiful."

Kimo and Noelani's final instruction to Peter was to "take care of our daughters." After many hugs, kisses, and tears, we boarded the plane.

Our flight from Honolulu to Salt Lake City was pleasantly uneventful, but I was grateful for the chance to move around a little once we landed. I hurried to the restroom while Peter went in search of coffee. He returned with two surprises—a pumpkin spice latte and a crumb cake. We had an hour and a half before our connecting flight, giving us much needed leisure time.

After about thirty minutes the announcement came that our flight was boarding. The plane was packed, and we couldn't be more appreciative Kimo upgraded our tickets to first class.

I woke up about an hour before we were scheduled to land. Peter was already awake and having a snack.

"Hi, honey," he said, smiling. "Are you hungry?"

"I sure am."

He touched my cheek. "You looked so peaceful. I didn't want to disturb you when the flight attendant brought drinks and snacks, but she said she'd bring you something when you awakened."

"Thanks," I said, stretching my back a little. "Would you order me a ginger ale and a cheese and fruit plate? I'm going to the restroom to freshen up."

I washed my face and reapplied a little makeup. My food had already arrived when I returned to my seat. Peter gave me a hug and patted my tummy.

"How's my little Samantha doing?"

I patted my tummy. "She's doing fine, Daddy."

"Let's pray before we land," he suggested. "I know you want everything to be perfect."

We joined hands and bowed our heads. Peter prayed that our time with Sam and my parents would be blessed and that Sam would be able to accompany us to my parents' house. He prayed Samantha and I would be well during our time on the mainland.

When we touched down in Salt Lake City, I wondered about my hero, Sam. Will he look different? Will he recognize me now that I'm pregnant? Will Sandy be with him?

Feeling fatigued, I held on to Peter as the moving sidewalk took us to the baggage claim where we were to meet Sam. Peter made me sit when we reached the baggage area, while he pushed his way into the group of people gathered around the baggage belt.

I squinted my eyes and spotted Sam and Sandy coming in

the outside door of the baggage claim, hurrying towards me. Sandy lunged at me knocking me back into the seat. Her wet tongue licked at my tears as I threw my arms around her. "Oh Sandy, I love you too."

"Well, lookie here, Sandy," Sam said. "Our little Lyndie is going to be a mommy."

I hugged Sam with all the strength I could muster. "Oh, I've missed you and Sandy so much." I broke into tears and sobbed into his chest. "I'm so sorry for all I did to you."

"I've missed you too," he said, his voice cracking. "No need to be sorry. God has turned everything around for good, like it says in the book of Romans."

Sam stepped out of our embrace when Peter approached, dragging our luggage behind him. "This must be your wonderful husband."

"Yes, sir, I am," Peter said, smiling. "And I'm pleased to finally meet Lyndie's rescuer and special friend."

Peter put out his hand, but Sam grabbed him and pulled him into a big hug instead. When Sam broke away, Sandy saw her chance and jumped up and licked Peter's face.

"I guess Sandy approves of you too," Sam teased.

We all laughed.

"I have a car out front," Sam said. "I borrowed a station wagon from one of my neighbors, so you and your bags would fit."

Sam took my arm, and Peter brought the baggage. "I'd like to take you folks to dinner," Sam said. "There's a terrific seafood restaurant right across the street from your hotel. I know my Lyndie loves seafood. I checked with the hotel, and they gave special permission for Sandy to stay in your room while we eat. I know she won't be happy about that, so to keep her busy, I brought her a bone."

The Harbor Seafood & Steak Company, a tasty high-end restaurant with linen tablecloths, was a refreshing change from the long airplane ride. I ordered coconut shrimp, Peter chose shrimp scampi, and Sam ordered grilled Alaskan salmon. Peter also ordered a large Greek salad for all of us to share.

"Do you mind if we sit for a moment?" Sam asked later as we entered our hotel room.

"Of course not," Peter said.

Sam brought out his Bible and pointed at how he recorded the day I left. He went on to show me scriptures he wrote down and prayed daily on my behalf. My parents had contacted him to tell him I wasn't on the plane when they went to meet me. After that, he fasted and stayed in constant prayer. He also kept in contact with my parents to pray and encourage them to trust God to bring me home.

"Sam, when I first saw Lyndie on the plane, I instantly fell in love with her. I knew from the moment I laid eyes on her that she was my forever. Someway, somehow, I was determined to make her mine. I'll finish my story tomorrow. Right now she needs to get some rest."

"I agree." Sam took my hand. "I want to let you know how honored I am to be include in the reunion with your family."

"Sam, I know if you are there, everything will work out well."

"I'm glad you guys decided to spend a day relaxing at my house before we fly out the following day to Washington, D.C. I think a day on the farm will be good for Lyndie."

"Looking forward to it."

We hugged and said our good-byes for the night.

Later, lying in Peter's arms, I thanked God for the blessed time with Sam.

≈ 22 ≈

The Homecoming

Our time with Sam was not only fun but inspirational. We couldn't stop laughing when Peter tried to feed the pigs. One chased him, and they both fell in the mud. The pig wallowed right next to him and pushed Peter with his snout.

I spent time in the barn brushing Daisy, who rubbed my cheek with her head. I whispered, "I told you, Daisy, that I'd come back to you and Sam and Sandy. I'm sorry I can't ride you, but I'm going to have a baby. Maybe my little girl can ride you someday. I love you, Daisy."

When we finished feeding the animals and the chores were done, we headed into the house and sat in the living room with Sandy lying by my feet. Sam pulled out his Bible, bowed his head, and prayed, "Lord, give me Your words that You want me to share with this couple."

He smiled. "Lyndie, your secret kept you in fear. Now that you've exposed the truth to God's love and grace, your fear, guilt, and hopelessness don't have a hold on you anymore. You know in Isaiah it says, 'no weapon that is fashioned against you shall succeed, and you shall refute every tongue that rises against you in judgment.' Use the Word of God against fear when it comes, and let the love of God help put your fears to rest."

The sincerity in Sam's voice brought tears to my eyes.

"Remember, God has a plan and purpose for your life, and it's good." Sam smiled and nodded. "He'll give you what you need to fulfill it."

I narrowed my eyes and studied Sam's face. He had the

same expression as my grandma had when she used to talk to me about God.

"That's a powerful word, Sam," Peter said.

Sam turned to Peter. "It says in the book of Ephesians that you are to love your wife as you love your own body, and to love her as Christ loves the church. You're commanded to wash her in the Word. Have you wondered why God put instructions to husbands about how to love their wives in this book and then ended it with instructions on how to put on the whole armor of God?"

Peter shook his head. "No, I never thought about that."

Sam put his hand on Peter's shoulder. "I believe that's because a husband is to not only teach the Word to his wife, but he is also to pray for strength for her in the unseen battles she will face."

His brow furrowed in obvious concentration, Peter leaned forward slightly and kept his eyes on Sam but kept silent.

"Peter," Sam continued, "your job is to protect your wife. Give her the shield of faith to deflect the arrows of doubt, fear, despair, or accusation. Put in her hand the sword of the Spirit—the Word of God—which gives her the strength to stand against anything that comes against her."

Tears shone in Peter's eyes as he drew me close to him.

"Sam, I'll do everything to love Lyndie the way the Bible instructs me to. And I promise to lift Lyndie up in prayer daily."

"Why don't you two lie down and take a nap? Tomorrow's going to be a busy day."

We agreed and quickly fell into a deep sleep. In a dream I saw a huge cross in front of me. As I continued to look at it, pieces of the cross chipped off one by one and fell at my feet. Each piece bore various words: pain, guilt, unworthiness, abuse, rejection. I looked up, and the cross glowed. Love like I'd never felt before emanated from that cross.

I awoke and sat up in bed, knowing what it meant. Jesus

took all my hurts on the cross and exchanged them with His love. Everything Sam had shared with me and all I learned the last months in Bible study came together in the dream. Something broke free inside me, and I felt strong. I realized I no longer had to live in my brokenness.

The next day Sam prepared quite a feast for us for supper: southern fried chicken and all the trimmings, including homemade cornbread. Sam's mom had been from the South, and Sam explained she often cooked this same meal for her family.

In the middle of the meal, Sam cautioned us, "Save some room for dessert. I made Lyndie's favorite carrot cake."

"Oh, Sam, thank you so much! I remember when you made that for my birthday. You make the absolute best carrot cake I've ever eaten. Please give me your recipe."

Later while Peter cleared the table then loaded and ran the dishwasher, Sam made decaf coffee and took out some paper plates. While we sat in the living room having cake and coffee, Sam showed Peter pictures of Sarah. Sandy sat with her head on my lap as I petted her.

"What an attractive woman with such a sweet smile," Peter observed.

"Yes, that was my darling," Sam said, a tinge of melancholy in his voice. "I miss her every day. But I know someday I'll be with her for all eternity."

Peter's brows knit together. "Sam, not only has this been an enjoyable time here with you today, but I've learned so much. And now there's something Lyndie and I have been meaning to ask you. Would you be Samantha's spiritual godfather? It's a special title we want you to have."

Sam's eyes twinkled as he nodded. "I would consider it a great honor. But there's something important I'd like you two to think about. Spending time with you made me miss not having a family. Sarah and I couldn't have children. I have no grandchildren. Lyndie's the closest thing I have to a daughter. You know,

I've had this here farm for a long time now, and I can still maintain the work. Yet, I've come to a time in my life I don't want to work hard anymore. I've been thinking about retiring somewhere, but I just didn't know where. Last night it came to me, if you'd have us, I'd like to move Sandy and me to Hawaii, somewhere close to you."

"Oh, Sam!" I jumped up and hugged him. "We don't have to think about that at all. In fact, my wish has always been the two men I love so dearly would always be close to me and now to my daughter."

"That's wonderful," Peter said, grinning. "And you'll be closer than you might have bargained for. If it's agreeable to you, we'll fix up the old groomer's cabin on our property for you and Sandy to live in. And you could help with the horses—and of course bring Daisy and Rocket with you."

Sam's face seemed to glow. "Done deal," he said. "One of my neighbors, who'll be keeping Sandy for me while I travel with you, offered to buy this place if I ever sell. He'll be overjoyed I finally decided to sell it to them."

Before Peter and I went back to our hotel, we all prayed and thanked God for working out the details of our lives. Later, in bed, Peter held me close. I fell asleep knowing God was truly ordering my steps.

Early the next morning we met Sam at Dulles International Airport giving Peter time to upgrade Sam's ticket to first class allowing all of us to sit together.

Peter and Sam checked us in, then we went through security, and I sat in the waiting area with Sam while Peter searched for a Starbucks to get us some breakfast.

"Got something for you," Sam said, handing me an envelope.

I turned it over to examine it. "What's this, Sam?"

"It's a letter from your mother. When you didn't get off the plane that day, your mother put her feelings into a letter for you.

She said if you contacted me to please make sure I got it to you. I believe now's the perfect time to give it to you."

Placing it in my pocket, "Thanks. I hope you don't mind if I wait to read it." As the plane took off, I pulled the envelope out.

"What's that?" Peter asked.

"A letter from my mother."

Peter put his hand on my arm. My hands shook as I opened the letter and read.

Dearest Lyndie,

God has placed a sacred bond between a mother and daughter that remains stronger than other family relationships. It is rooted in unconditional love. In my heart, I knew you were still alive. Often, I went into your room, held your stuffed teddy bear, and prayed. It made me feel close to you. I never gave up hope. Instead, I trusted God was taking care of you. One of the agents at the FBI periodically constructed an age-enhanced photo for me of what you might look like now. I kept these photos with me. Over time, your dad lost hope, especially after prayers and well wishes from friends began to dwindle. His heart grew sick. When the call came from Sam you were alive, it renewed his faith. Although you weren't on the plane when we went to the airport to pick you up, we both agreed God had indeed answered our prayers. We believed you would return home, and we waited with open arms full of love and acceptance. You are my darling daughter.

Love,
Mom

I wiped a tear from my cheek.

Peter squeezed my arm. "You all right, honey?"

"Yes, I'm better than all right. All my fear is gone. My mother loves me no matter what."

He took my hand. "Now let's try to get some rest." It wasn't long before we all dozed off.

Peter gently aroused me from my sleep. "We'll be landing in about an hour. The flight attendants are taking final orders for drinks or snacks, and they'll be bringing around a hot towel."

"Thanks." I tried to stretch. My back hurt from sleeping curled up on the seat. "I probably should go use the restroom and freshen up a bit. Why don't you order me orange juice and some crackers and cheese?"

When I returned to my seat, my order was already there. I ate quickly as I knew it wouldn't be long until we landed.

Sam glanced at us from across the aisle. "Let's thank God for getting us here safely and for this blessed celebration that we're about to experience."

When we looked up from prayer, the flight attendant was handing out the hot towels. I gratefully accepted one, and it felt wonderful and helped relieve the tightness in my neck from the trip.

Time seemed to float in slow motion as we entered the terminal.

"Peter! Look!" I cried, grabbing onto him, my legs buckling.

Mom and Dad stood near the gate. I later learned my brother, now an airline pilot, explained our story to airport security and received special clearance to let my parents come to the gate. They looked exactly the same—older, but the same. I focused on their teary smiles.

Tears spilled from my eyes as well, and my heart skipped a beat at seeing my family again. They ran to me and smothered me with kisses. Then I fell into my mother's arms. My dad, Sam, and Peter stood off to the side and gave us this moment— a moment that will forever be etched in my memory.

"Oh, Lyndie, my precious daughter!" Mom cried. "I knew God would keep you alive, and I would hold you once again."

Dad swallowed a sob as he stepped up to join us. "Your mother never gave up hope. She refused to listen to anyone who wouldn't believe as she did." He threw his arms around both of us.

After what seemed an eternity, my dad broke free, and I realized I needed to introduce everyone.

"Mom," I said, pulling back from our hug, "this is my husband, Peter."

Mom kissed Peter on the cheek and hugged him. Then she turned to Sam. "You must be Sam. You're our hero. You saved my daughter."

Sam's face flushed. "No, ma'am. Jesus saved her. I was just glad to be able to help."

My dad hugged Peter and Sam. "You're both part of our family now."

"Come on, sweetheart," he said, taking my hand. "Let's go home."

☞23☜

Family

Peter sat in the front seat with my dad. I sat behind them between my mother and Sam. Both held my hands on the way home.

"Your brother and his family are waiting at the house," Mom said, squeezing my hand.

My brother! I calculated how old he'd be now. I'd been gone about eleven years, and he was twelve when I was taken, which meant he was about twenty-three. I tried to imagine what Tommy might look like now.

Our little town hadn't changed much. The village drugstore, veterinarian hospital, and my elementary school still stood, basically unchanged, on Main Street. All the buildings seemed smaller. The trees in the park looked bigger than I remembered them. The town even had a Starbucks now.

I wasn't expecting what awaited me at my parents' home. Balloons and streamers were strung across the front porch, and a big welcome-home sign decorated the front door.

As we pulled up, the front door opened, and a familiar looking young man rushed out onto the front porch, a war of emotions playing across his face. My heart leapt with recognition. I studied him for a moment and realized he looked just as I imagined he would. We nearly fell into each other's arms, and the years we'd been apart faded.

Tommy introduced me to his wife, Jennifer, a petite blonde with big brown eyes and a cute, upturned nose. Her warm hug and kiss, along with her bubbly personality immediately captured my heart. I could see why Tommy had fallen in love with her.

And then I met their children—Jacob, three, and Rachel, one—and my heart swelled with joy as I realized I had a niece and a nephew.

Mom had prepared all the food I loved as a child—platters of cheese ravioli, spaghetti with garlic and oil, Caesar salad, garlic parmesan cheese bread, homemade applesauce, and of course my favorite cookies—peanut butter.

"Sam, would you mind saying the blessing for us?" Mom asked.

"My pleasure. Dear Lord, thank You for reuniting this beautiful family and letting me be part of it. Let the food nourish our bodies and bless the hands that prepared it."

Mom smiled. "That was beautiful. We want to thank you for all you did for Lyndie."

"It blessed me to do it," he responded.

"I prayed and prayed and never doubted God would one day return our daughter to us." Steve, my dad, chimed in. "I fought desperately to hold on to my faith after Lyndie's abduction. With each passing year, I lost hope and my heart grew heavy, like it says in the book of Proverb. Thanks to your phone call, Sam, my hope was renewed."

Sam nodded. "We always have to trust and hold on to our faith."

My dad surprised us with a treat after dinner. He brought out a DVD he'd converted from old movies of Tommy and me when we were little. I watched my brother running after me trying to pull my pigtails. Memories of my time at home with my brother flooded back into my mind, happy times that gave me hope and comfort while I was in captivity. Peter made comments about how cute a little girl I was, and Tommy agreed. Watching the movies with everyone, laughing and reminiscing, spread a feeling of warmth through me.

This is the moment I waited for. I'm home with my family! I patted my stomach. Soon there'll be another member of this family present.

After we finished watching the movie, my mother beckoned me to come with her. I followed her upstairs to my old room. I felt as though I'd stepped back in time. My favorite color as a child was lavender. My blue and lavender bedspread still covered my bed. My childhood teddy bear, Bear Bear, sat on my dresser. He seemed to be smiling at me.

I looked around the room, and in one corner stood the vintage rocker Mom sat in to read me stories at night. On the far-right wall was the desk where I used to sit for hours, writing and illustrating stories, dreaming of being an author when I grew up. Sitting on the desk was a picture of my grandmother. For a moment I remembered the feel of her arms, the smell of her hair. I could almost hear her say to me, "Lyndie, God's plans for you are good."

I swallowed a lump in my throat and blinked tears from my eyes.

On my bookshelf I spotted the book my mom used to read to me when I was little, *Noah and the Rainbow*. I picked it up and sat on my bed. Mom joined me and pulled me into her arms. Tears glistened in her eyes as she said, "I remember this was your favorite book. You wanted me to read it to you every night before bed. That's why I kept it right where it was. Soon I can read it to your daughter."

I closed my eyes, drinking in the moment with my mother. Then without warning a cold chill swept over me, and a horrible image from the past flashed in my mind. My stomach retched as I looked into the face of one of my abusers. I could almost feel his rough hands on my skin.

No, I screamed inwardly. *I belong to Jesus now. You will not ruin this moment.* My entire body trembled, as Mom stroked my head.

"It's okay," she said. "Honey, you're home. No one will ever hurt you again."

She pulled me close and held me until I relaxed. "I saved

everything that was yours as a child. I knew in my heart you'd return. I also prayed one day you'd have a daughter of your own, and all your childhood things could be hers. My prayers certainly have been answered."

I sniffled and managed a smile. "Thanks a bunch, Mom. I'll look at these things tomorrow if it's okay. It's been quite an evening, and I'm pretty exhausted."

She nodded. "Of course. I've fixed the guest room for you and Peter. Tommy's old room will be for Sam. I think he'll be quite comfortable there."

Back downstairs, Peter looked at me pleadingly. "Honey, you look so tired. Tomorrow's another day. I need to get you to bed."

"I'm ready," I admitted. "It's been an emotional day." After a series of good nights, kisses, and hugs, we finally made it to bed.

"Thank You, Jesus," was my last prayer that night. A moment later, I was asleep.

Peter and I slept in, grateful no one got us up early. When I finally opened my eyes, I flipped the covers back and stood. I squinted in the sunlight streaming through the window. I stretched, feeling calm and relaxed, I slipped my robe on, and pushed my feet into the fuzzy slippers my mom had leant me. I felt as warm and secure as my feet in the slippers. I'm home.

The aroma of blueberry pancakes filled my senses, another of my special favorites. Jennifer, Jacob, and Rachel were already enjoying them as I walked into the kitchen.

My mother looked up, "How'd you sleep, honey?"

"Like a baby. Where's Peter?"

"He, Sam, Tommy, and your dad all went into town to get some supplies. They want to have a barbecue and a bonfire tonight. They should be back shortly."

Mom flipped a pancake, then put some on a plate, which she handed to me, along with a bottle of syrup. I took a bite of one of the pancakes and smacked my lips.

"Isn't that yummy syrup?" Mom asked. "Your Aunt Betsy in Paradise, Michigan, sent that for Christmas. Her family makes syrup from their very own maple trees." She smiled. "I think I'm going to make us another cup of tea."

"Sounds good, Mom. Can we take the drinks out on the front porch? I'd like to talk."

"Sure. Go ahead. I'll be right out."

In minutes, we were both settled on the porch swing, our hands wrapped around steaming cups of tea.

"Would it be uncomfortable for you if we talked about that day in New York City?"

"No, not at all. I looked forward to that mother-daughter outing for a long time. Remember how excited I got when we went to see the Christmas tree at Rockefeller Center?"

Mom nodded and smiled. "Yes, and it started snowing. It was like a Christmas movie."

"Oh, and we can't forget FAO Schwartz, the legendary toy store. Grandma told me about it when I was a little girl. I never saw so many toys ... and the giant teddy bear at the entrance. It all seemed magical, especially when we watched the Christmas show at Radio City Music Hall. My favorite part was the Rockettes. I remember you let me take a picture with them."

Mom got up, a subtle grin on her face. "I'll be right back."

When she returned, she handed me a portrait. "Here, I saved it for you."

I closed my eyes and held it against my heart. "This is wonderful, Mom. I can't tell you how many times, during my darkest moments, I'd picture you and me and the fun we had in New York City. Though that day changed my life, I want you to know I forever cherish those memories."

Tears shone in Mom's eyes. "Thanks for sharing that. At times I blamed myself for taking you to the city. When you were taken, it hurt really bad. The pain immobilized me mentally and physically. I had to let go, give it to God, and trust him. My faith pushed me through the pain of losing you."

Tears also stung my eyes and spilled over onto my face. "I'm sorry, Mom. I should have listened to you. You warned me about Anthony. He took advantage of my innocence. I mistook his attention for him liking me. How stupid I was to let him deceive me."

She laid her hand on my arm. "No, you're not to blame. You reacted like any typical teenage girl would. He fooled you with his charm. I should have been firmer with my warnings."

I swallowed the lump in my throat. "The good thing is, I'm home now."

"Yes, God brought you back to me."

We looked up to see the men pull into the driveway. Peter came over and wrapped his arms around my shoulders, leaned down, and kissed me.

"How are my girls today?" he said, patting my stomach.

"We're just fine, Daddy."

We spent the afternoon hanging around the house with the family. Jacob brought out all his cars and Legos, and Peter sat on the floor in the living room playing with him. Rachel kept climbing into my lap with her teddy bear and wanted to play with my hair. "Perty, perty," she said.

I enjoyed getting to know my family again. The joy I experienced reminded me of Christmas morning. I couldn't stop smiling or telling them how good it was to be home where I belong. I'm a part of them. My mom's eyes shone with a love I had longed for as a captive teenager. Her unconditional love made me feel safe and secure.

Mom also told me she worked at the church nursery school after I disappeared. I was glad to know she could give her love to those children but sad those years were stolen from us. She said she volunteered once a week at a homeless shelter now, and I was proud to have a mother who so generously gave herself to others.

My dad was kind and loving, just as I remembered him. He

openly showed my mom affection and hugged me and told me he loved me several times a day. After leaving his government job, he'd continued his career as a lawyer and did well for himself as senior partner in the company.

Tommy worked for United Airlines and loved traveling the world. His wife was a licensed cosmetologist but now a stay-at-home mom.

Jennifer and I sat together in the living room. She told me my mom had taken up quilt-making, showing me a memory quilt Mom had created of some of my special outfits—my first onesie, first Easter dress, overalls, baby bonnets, first blanket, and my Hello Kitty play outfit.

Mom walked in from the kitchen as I admired the quilt. I grabbed her hands. "Mom, I love the memory quilt! You need to promise to teach me how to quilt."

While we women chatted about sewing, the men offered to make dinner. Sam started the barbecue, and Dad seasoned the meat. Peter made macaroni salad and potato salad and was just starting on the baked beans when Mom yelled from the living room, "Hey, Peter, don't forget to put some maple syrup in the beans."

Later we took advantage of the warm July night and ate on the back porch. Memories of my childhood on the porch danced through my mind. I blinked away a tear, thinking back on how happy and carefree my life was then. I could almost see Tommy and myself running around catching fireflies. As I sat there that evening, enjoying the company of my loved ones, I thought, *I'm making new memories.*

Sam lit the firepit on the porch, and Peter surprised me with marshmallows. "Lyndie told me one of favorite memories growing up was making smores with you, Tommy."

"I remember Lyndie would smear the marshmallows on the chocolate, but she always managed to have just as much chocolate on her face."

Everyone chuckled at Tommy's remark, while enjoying the messy treat, especially the two little ones.

Jacob ran up to me with a jar. "I taught Jacob how to collect fireflies like we did when we were kids." I put my hand on my precious nephew's head. He giggled every time a firefly lit up.

As we sat around the bonfire laughing and talking, Dad clapped his hands and bellowed, "I need everyone's attention. I have an important announcement to make."

⤳24⤝

Dad's Surprise

"Peter, Sam and I have been talking. Sam shared with me he's selling his farm and moving to Kauai, and I started thinking. When I got home today, I talked my idea over with your mom, and she confessed she'd been thinking about the same thing." He winked at me. "I'll be sixty soon, you know, and I'm ready to retire. Our house is paid for, and it's time to downsize."

My parents exchanged smiles across the room before Dad went on. "We've decided to purchase a two-bedroom condo here and also invest in a small home on Kauai."

My hand flew to my mouth.

"This way we can spend half our time with our grandchildren here," Dad explained, "and the other half with our grandchildren in Hawaii. As you know we have flying privileges, thanks to Tommy."

My lower lip quivered, and my eyes filled with tears. I couldn't restrain my joy for another minute. I threw my arms around my parents.

"Oh, I'm so excited!" I declared, looking back and forth from one parent to the other. "You've truly made my dreams come true. Now I'll have all the people I love around me. I may have missed out on the love of a family for many years, but God is restoring what I lost, just like it says in Joel 2:25, 'And I will restore to you the years that the swarming locust hath eaten.'"

Tears of joy dripped down my face. "He is such a loving God, and now I know Samantha will grow up surrounded with a loving family. He gave me back everything I lost and more than I could ever have imagined."

The following morning the guys went to show off the town to Sam and Peter. When they returned, Peter divulged the news. They'd gotten Mom, me, and Jennifer gift cards for a spa.

"Everyone deserves a little pampering now and then," Peter winked.

We left Jacob and Rachel with the men, thrilled and eager for an afternoon of beauty. When we entered the luxurious spa, I looked around, awestruck. I'd never seen such a place before.

We showed our certificates, and the attendant handed us ultra-luxe, double-layer microfiber robes and slippers. She offered us a selection of fresh juices, savory teas, and healthy snacks while we waited. We chose the spa special package, which included a deluxe facial and a massage.

After the facial, our skin glowed. The low lighting, soothing music, and the aromatherapy oils in the serenity lounge encouraged deep relaxation. What a wonderful experience for us ladies!

On the drive home, Mom surprised us, "Let's stop at Macy's. I want to buy you girls a gift."

She bought me a new maternity pantsuit and Jennifer a black leather purse.

"Mom, you are such a blessing."

By the time we arrived home, the men had prepared supper—a vegetable lasagna with parmesan cheese and fresh garlic bread. Sam spoiled us with an English Trifle dessert.

After dinner we sat around in the family room contemplating our new adventure with all the family on Kauai. We also discussed our plan for the next day. Everyone wanted to go to the bay to watch the Fourth of July fireworks. Tommy suggested we spend the afternoon at the zoo and go out to eat before the firework display. We all agreed that sounded like fun, especially for the little ones. Peter and I turned in early, knowing we were in for a busy day.

The next morning, we headed to the zoo in perfect seventy-degree weather. Jennifer put the children in a double stroller, but Jacob kept wanting out to get closer to the animals.

Peter tried to get me to sit down and rest, but I assured him I was fine. I told him about an article I recently read in the *New York Times,* which stated that a mother's exercise can boost the development of her unborn child's brain. Still not convinced, he insisted I rest periodically. To be honest I enjoyed the way he coddled me.

When I stood up after one rest, I noticed a young couple with a baby girl. "Look how cute that family is," I said.

Peter kissed my cheek. "Honey, that's going to be us soon."

We ate lunch at a small outdoor restaurant near the black bear caves, my favorite exhibit. We sat while Dad ordered hot dogs, chips, and fresh-squeezed lemonade for all of us.

Right before we finished eating, Jacob yelled. "Take me to grafs."

I giggled at the way he tried to say giraffe, but soon we were standing in front of the giraffe exhibit as Jacob climbed up on the platform to try to be as tall as the giraffes. When it was time to move on, he started crying, not wanting to leave.

"Let's go see the monkeys." Jennifer said, switching his attention to the next exhibit.

Jacob imitated the monkey faces, and we laughed until our faces hurt. Then Peter bought a bag of salted peanuts to feed the elephants, but I ate most of them before we got to that exhibit. I couldn't resist the tasty treat. I'd craved salt ever since I got pregnant.

Peter's cellphone rang. "It's my parents," he said, putting the phone on speaker.

"How's our Lyndie feeling?" Kimo asked.

"She's doing fine." A huge grin spread over Peter's face. "And I have awesome news. Lyndie's parents decided to get a place in Kauai. They'll stay there for half the year."

"Oh, Peter," Kimo said as Noelani squealed with delight,

"we've been praying for this. God has answered our prayer for Lyndie to have her family close now they're back in her life."

"There's a great soup-and-salad restaurant called The Kettle," suggested Jennifer, "my friends rave about their fresh salads and wide varieties of soup, but their homemade bread and different flavored butters made it famous."

"Sounds good to me," I said, and everyone nodded.

We left the zoo around five-thirty to get to the restaurant by six. It turned out to be everything Jennifer had promised. On the main wall stood a big brick fireplace, which gave it a homey atmosphere, along with the cozy booths. With such a large assortment of soups, it was difficult to choose which one to order.

I decided on both the corn chowder and New England clam chowder. The waitress brought a basket of homemade hot breads, with garlic and honey butter to our table. While I enjoyed my chowders, Peter ate three bowls of broccoli cheddar soup.

We left an hour later and drove to an open field behind the high school to park. Peter took my hand, and we all went to find a good spot to view the fireworks.

"Maybe I'll walk off some of these calories from all the bread I ate," I quipped.

Peter smiled and patted my tummy. My dad and Sam carried our folding chairs for us. Dad found a good place to watch the fireworks. He and Sam set up the chairs, and we all sat down while Jacob and Rachel stayed in their strollers.

As the display began, Jacob kept saying, "Oooo, look! I like that one. Perty one!"

The grand finale was the most impressive, with fireworks in the shape and colors of the American flag, while the Veteran band played the Star-Spangled Banner.

The children fell asleep on the way home, and I had a hard time keeping my eyes open. When we got to the house, Peter fixed hot cocoa with peanut butter cookies for us before we went to sleep.

Dad's Surprise

Knowing we had only a few more days with my parents, we spent most of our time at the house. Peter helped my dad work on the car he was restoring, a '49 Ford Woody Wagon. Sam spent time with Tommy looking at his travel photographs and talking about the places he traveled. Mom gave Jennifer and me quilting lessons, while Rachel and Jacob played with scraps of material on the sewing room floor.

Our three-week vacation came to an end far too soon. On the drive to the airport, I held tightly to my mother's hand as tears stung my eyes. This time they were tears of joy, knowing we'd be together again soon.

We all hugged Sam goodbye as his flight departed first.

My mother took his hand. "We love you, Sam. You're family."

I thanked God for His love and the love of my family. Although it was difficult to say our goodbyes, we were happy that soon my parents would be living close by, and they'd be part of our child's life.

On the flight home, Peter took my hand. "Sweetheart, this was such a beautiful celebration with Sam and your parents and Tommy's family. I'm honored to be part of it and to see how the Lord took care of you all this time for this very moment. He deserves all the glory for this blessed reunion."

I nodded. "Yes, He does. God is so good!"

As I shifted in the seat, a sharp pain radiated towards my abdomen. I took short quick breaths until the discomfort subsided.

Peter frowned. "Are you all right?"

"I'm fine," I promised him.

Looking only somewhat reassured he said, "Try to get some rest, honey. You look exhausted."

When we arrived at Honolulu International Airport, we had only a fifty-minute wait until our flight to Lihue. My body jolted when another sharp pain ran down my lower back down the back of my leg.

"Are you sure everything is okay with the baby?" Peter questioned.

"I'm just over-fatigued. I can't wait to get home and into my own bed."

Kimo picked us up at the airport while Noelani waited at home. I fell asleep listening to Peter and his dad chatting about the trip. I was extremely tired when we arrived at our place. I don't even remember climbing into bed.

———

The next several months were busy with doctor appointments, fixing up the nursery for Samantha, and getting the guest house ready for Sam. Kimo and Noelani helped. My mother and Sam called every day to check on us and to share their love.

One day Noelani exploded into our house with amazing news. "Hey, you two, you'd better sit down. Wait until I tell you the miracle God did today. Peter, do you remember the Kamalis, the older couple who live down the road? Well, today they stopped by to tell me they're considering selling their home sometime this year and moving to Oahu. They think they'd like to be closer to their son and grandchildren. Their house is a two-bedroom with a den that could be used for an office. It would be perfect for your parents, Lyndie!"

"Slow down now, Mom," Peter chuckled. "You're getting a little ahead of yourself, don't you think?"

"Well, I thought it sounded promising," Noelani said, grinning sheepishly.

———

Four weeks before my delivery date, I awoke with persistent pain in my abdomen and a fever of 101. Peter rushed me to the ER, and Noelani phoned my obstetrician who said he'd meet us there.

After examining me and running tests, Dr. Klein admitted me to the hospital. He came into my room and announced, "You have a bacterial infection. I'm putting you on a regime of antibiotics." Doctor Klein avoided my gaze and looking at the clipboard in his hand he said, "Peter, the infection could be dangerous to the placenta, lead to birth abnormalities, or make labor harmful and difficult. Also, the fetus seems to be in distress. I am recommending an emergency cesarean section."

A surge of fear overtook me, and I started to tremble and cry. "Oh, Peter, I'm so scared. I don't want anything to happen to our baby."

He held me close. "We need to trust God. Your parents are on a flight here, and the Stangels and my parents and Sam just came to pray with us."

Sure enough, when Peter opened the door, they all filed into the room. We immediately joined hands and bowed our heads. "Father God," Pastor Stangel prayed, "guide the hands of the doctor today. We ask you to keep Lyndie and Samantha safe during the operation, and we thank you for a healthy child. In Jesus' name, amen."

The nurse along with the anesthesiologist came in then and asked everyone to leave. They needed to prep me. My C-section was urgent and general anesthesia was used. There was no time for an epidural.

Moments later, in a whirl of commotion, they were wheeling me into the operating room.

The next thing I knew, I woke up, in desperate need of water. "I need something to drink," I managed to say.

The nurse gave me ice chips. "You might vomit if we give you water," she explained.

I became aware of a warm hand holding mine. I squinted, and Peter's face came into focus.

"Hi, sweetheart," he said softly. "How are you feeling?"

"Like I've been sawed in half. How's Samantha?"

He smiled. "She's doing well. The doctor put her in the Neonatal Intensive Care Unit because she has jaundice. She needs phototherapy to get rid of the bilirubin that causes jaundice."

My heart skipped a beat. "I don't want my baby to be sick on account of me."

He squeezed my hand. "It's not your fault," he assured me. "And right now, we just need you to get better."

The nurse appeared with a wheelchair then. "Do you think you'd like to see your daughter? You can view her through the glass right now. Tomorrow you should be able to hold her."

I was thrilled. In moments I was staring at the most beautiful baby I'd ever seen. "She looks like you," I told Peter, though he countered that she was the spitting image of her beautiful mother.

That night in the maternity ward, I woke myself up with a scream, covered in sweat and breathing heavily. I looked around, trying to get a sense of where I was. Two nurses rushed in and calmed me down, assuring me I'd had a bad dream.

I knew better. It wasn't just a bad dream. It was a nightmarish horror. The suffocating stench of a dirty room, the groans of shackled girls who stretched their arms toward me. In my dream, I stood immobilized, unable to help them.

Peter, who'd slept on a cot in my room, had already climbed onto my bed. Lying down next to me, he stroked my hair and spoke soothingly to me. "It's going to be all right, sweetheart. I'm here with you. No one is going to hurt you."

"But this wasn't like those accusing and condemning dreams I had before," I explained, my breathing starting to normalize. "I saw real girls, victims of human trafficking. They were pleading with me to help them."

"Honey, you've been through a lot the last few days, and you could also be experiencing the effect of the drugs they gave you."

I shook my head. "No, Peter. It was real. I saw the terror on their faces."

"Okay. Then let's pray for them to be rescued."

The memory of my agonizing dream was almost forgotten the next day when the neonatal pediatrician delivered devastating news. "Samantha's staying in the NICU due to respiratory distress. I've put her on antibiotics to prevent sepsis or pneumonia. And of course, she's on all manner of surveillance monitoring. But we'll let you breastfeed her later today."

Various emotions wrestled inside me, as I struggled to accept the doctor's words. All I'd wanted was a healthy baby. Now I felt like a helpless outsider, disconnected from my own child in the NICU.

My attempt to breastfeed Samantha that evening was unsuccessful, and the doctor discouraged me from trying again until day six. Bilirubin, jaundice, phototherapy, ventilator, icolet—we weren't prepared for the challenges, vocabulary, or high-level of technology in the NICU. But Samantha's fragile condition and her frequent crises were the hardest to handle. Both sets of our parents stayed by our side daily, praying and encouraging us.

My mother reassured me Samantha was a gift from God, and she was in his hands. My head knew that was true, but my heart still had doubts. I spent quite a bit of time in the hospital's chapel, with my mother at my side.

My infection soon cleared up, and after three days my doctor discharged me—a mother leaving the hospital without a baby. My baby's needs were being met by equipment and by others. Leaving without her left Peter and me with an unfulfilled birth experience and fear our baby could die.

At home we worried about any unanticipated crisis that might occur in our absence. We spent most of our time in the NICU and found it difficult to continue with the realities of life at home. The neonatal staff did their best to make us feel comfortable, as they were trained to take care of the family as well as the child.

God's grace and strength carried us through that tough time.

Samantha came home six days later, and it was like she knew where she belonged. She fit right into our lives, and she nursed until she was eighteen months old.

———•———

I couldn't have asked for a more perfect life. My parents eventually purchased the house Noelani had told us about, surrounding Samantha with those who loved her—two sets of grandparents, godfather Sam, and, of course, our church family. She was my little angel, and with her bouncy blonde curls and deep blue eyes, she resembled one too.

Samantha grew into a lovable and kind little toddler. She loved all of God's creatures, and we often found her sitting and singing to the birds in the trees in our yard. Her favorite thing was going with Peter and me to the beach. She'd laugh when the waves tickled her toes. And we'd hold her by her hands and lift her up to jump over them.

During the next twenty months, Peter and I couldn't have been more content. Yet a nagging uneasiness tugged at my heart. Several nights a week the nightmare I'd experienced in the maternity ward tormented my sleep. Peter dreaded the screams and the night terrors as much as I did.

In my dream I continued to hear the cries of young girls locked in cages, begging for my help. I felt their fear, and the haunting dreams continued. Peter finally insisted I get some help. He contacted Pastor Stangel and Karen to set up a time for me to counsel with them.

⁓25⁓

Another Blessing

On the day of my appointment to see the Stangels, I started throwing up profusely. Peter assumed I had the flu and sent me to bed, then rescheduled my appointment. The following day as the vomiting continued, he drove me to the clinic.

The doctor examined me and took a series of tests. After what seemed an eternity, he re-entered the little room where Peter and I sat. He smiled. "Well, I've found out what's wrong with you, and I think you're going to be very happy."

Peter and I glanced at each other. "You mean ...?"

The doctor nodded. "Your wife is pregnant."

Peter threw his arms around me and hugged me until I couldn't breathe, even as tears welled in my eyes. Another child!

Oh, thank You, Jesus, I prayed silently. Minutes later we were in our car driving to Peter's parents' home. We couldn't wait to tell our families and Sam the blessed news.

As soon as we walked into Noelani's house, she took one look at our faces and exclaimed, "Okay, you two, out with it. What's up? Why are you beaming like that?"

"Lyndie's pregnant," Peter announced. "We're going to have another child!"

Noelani grabbed me and held me close as Kimo entered the house, stopped, and took in the scene. "What's going on here?"

Noelani told him the news.

"Wonderful!" he said, giving me a hug and then turning to hug his son. "I hope this time it's a boy."

My parents showed up with Samantha. They kept her while

161

Peter and I were at the doctor. Samantha ran to us and I blurted out, "A boy, Peter and I are having a son!"

Mom and Dad threw their arms around me at the same time. "Oh, I'm so happy for you both," Dad said. "I'm going to be a grandmother again, praise God."

"What's all the excitement?' Sam asked as he walked in.

"Lyndie's pregnant. I'm having a son."

"Congratulations."

"This calls for a celebration," Kimo said. "Let's have a barbecue tonight and invite the Stangels and some of our friends from church."

We all applauded his idea and began preparing for the party. That evening as we all sat around the lanai, we enjoyed a time filled with laughter, tears, merriment, and prayer as we bowed our heads and Pastor Stangel thanked God for all the good he'd brought into our lives.

After we prayed, our pastor opened his Bible and read from the book of Romans: "And we know that in all things God works for the good of those who love him, who have been called according to his purpose." Then he looked up and explained, "No matter how much pain and suffering we encounter in life, God works all things together for our good."

As usual our daughter was the center of attention. Each person held Samantha and tickled her with kisses, while we sat around the firepit singing praise songs.

As the night grew late, Peter and I decided to go for a walk on the beach in front of his parents' house.

"You make me happier every day of our lives," Peter said, squeezing my hand.

"And you, my dear husband, bring more joy into my life than I ever hoped for or dared to imagine. My life is so very blessed."

Peter stood behind me, his arms around my waist, as we stared out at the ocean, glinting in the moonlight. It was truly an enchanted evening with the sound of the surf and a bright full moon overhead.

"I agree with my dad," Peter murmured. "I'm hoping it's a boy too."

I smiled up at him. "I'm just praying for a healthy baby."

"What would you name our baby if it's a boy?"

I hadn't thought of that yet. "Maybe we could give him a Hawaiian name, or name him after you or your dad."

"I was thinking of the name Caleb. In the Bible, Caleb was a man of faith who believed God and gave a good report after he went out with the other men to spy out the land."

I thought for a moment, "I like the name Caleb too. Let's pray about that, honey. First the doctors will have to determine it's a boy. If it's a girl I'd like to name her Ruth, after my mom. Ruth is one of my favorite women in the Bible. She was an extraordinarily strong woman."

Peter nodded. "I agree. That's a nice name for a girl, and it would truly bless your mom. How about Ruth Grace since it's God's grace that sustains us?"

"Great idea, sweetheart. I love it."

For the next several months, Peter waited in expectation of the news of our second child's sex. During this period, we watched our adorable toddler grow into a cute little girl. She didn't just walk—she ran everywhere. When she started talking, her vocabulary flourished. She could say Mommy, Daddy, Tutu, and Tutu Kani (the Hawaiian names for grandma and grandpa). She called my parents Pop Pop and Nana. And of course, Sam was just Sam.

Now that Samantha was mobile, she and Sandy became inseparable. He followed her everywhere, guarding and protecting her. Samantha loved the nursery at church, and we laughed every time she'd march around the house singing "Fadda Adaham."

The day finally arrived for my ultrasound appointment. We

prayed before entering the doctor's office, telling God how thankful we were and asking for a healthy baby. We told him we'd love whatever he chose to bless us with.

As the doctor ran the ultrasound wand over my tummy, he chuckled. "Well, you guys, now you need a nursery full of planes, trucks, and cars."

Peter beamed from ear to ear and puffed out his chest.

"I'm so happy for you, sweetheart. I know you wanted a son."

"Let's thank God right now," he said. Not waiting for the doctor to leave, we bowed our heads and thanked God for answering our prayers.

The next several months were a whirlwind of preparing for the birth of our son, whom we decided to name Caleb Peter. Noelani painted a mural on the nursery wall of Daniel in the lion's den. Peter put up shelves full of cars, trucks, and planes, just as the doctor had suggested. My mother gave me a baby shower, and between Sam and our families buying out the stores, we received everything we could possibly need. We were so busy with my doctor appointments and getting ready for the arrival of our son that I'd almost forgotten my nightmarish dreams.

ᗉ26ᗏ

The Nightmares Continue

A few nights before Caleb's due date, the haunting dream returned, this time more real than ever, as young girls called out to me, "Help us! Help us!" This time not only were they in filthy cages, but some were even shackled on dirty mattresses.

Peter heard me crying out and woke me. "What's the matter, sweetheart? Are you and the baby all right?"

"Oh, Peter," I sobbed, "it's those young girls again, pleading for my help. It was so real. I could see their faces and feel their pain."

"Honey, it was just a dream. We're going to go see Karen and Pastor Stangel tomorrow."

As it turned out, God had other plans for us. I started having contractions during breakfast, and by lunchtime we were headed for the hospital and they were eight minutes apart. I was grateful the labor progressed normally, and Caleb Peter was born three hours later, weighing seven pounds, three ounces. He had blue eyes and a full head of dark hair.

When I returned to my hospital room, our families, Sam, and the Stangels piled in. Everyone had something to say about Caleb's features, but the final consensus was that he resembled both of us.

While our parents and Sam prepared to leave, I noticed the pastors lingered behind. They stepped out in the hall when the nurse brought Caleb and placed him in my arms to nurse. Peter called them in when I finished, and Pastor Stangel prayed for Caleb, Peter, and me.

"Peter told me you're repeatedly having a disturbing dream.

After you're home and settled in, please come and meet with Karen and me. I might be able to give you some insight."

I nodded. "Thank you, Pastor. I look forward to getting together with you both."

Fatigue overtook me, and I was in my bed listening to my husband's slow breathing as he lay on a cot in the room, enjoying the peaceful solitude. Although I adored my family and their endearing affection, I welcomed being alone in the stillness of the night. During these times I felt the Lord closer, and I was filled with His peace.

Looking over at my handsome husband, I smiled as I admired his features. His face, with its strong mountain-peak cheekbones, accentuated his mariner blue eyes. Every time Peter looked at me with those spellbinding eyes, I melted. His sun-streaked sandy blond hair was casually jumbled on his forehead. I laughed to myself as I realized my man was desperately in need of a haircut. His Spartan-like physique always made me feel protected and safe.

I must have drifted off to sleep. The next thing I remember was the sound of someone sobbing, softly at first but growing in volume and intensity. Then I heard the snap of a whip, and girls screaming.

"Please, don't!" one voice cried. "Don't beat me anymore. I'll do whatever you say."

Another young girl whispered, "Help us, Lyndie! Help us, Lyndie!"

A deep voice emanated from something powerful—like a thundering waterfall. "Yes, Lyndie. You can help them."

Even though this voice seemed to shake the entire room, peace and familiarity also resonated from it.

"Wake up, Lyndie," a woman's voice said. "Are you all right?"

I opened my eyes to see my nurse standing over me, and I rubbed away the sleep.

"You were yelling," she said, "and we didn't want you to frighten the other patients."

I rolled my head to the side and saw Peter standing next to the bed. He took my hand and whispered, "I'm here, sweetheart. I'm here." The nurse left then, and Peter held my hand and stroked my hair until I fell back to sleep.

On the following day, Caleb came home, smothered with affection just like his sister. Samantha quickly became a little mother to Caleb. She was very protective of him and loved to tickle the bottom of his tiny feet and make him laugh. More than once we caught her in the nursery, reading him stories she made up from the pictures in her books. My tender-hearted daughter often sat by his crib, singing him songs until he fell asleep.

Peter and I sensed a strong bond developing between little brother and big sister, and it warmed our hearts. It reminded me of my brother, Tommy, and me when we were little. I decided our loving God was restoring my lost time with my brother.

The mysterious, majestic voice of the man in my dreams continued to nag at my heart and mind. It was as if the voice was of someone close—like a relative from the past. The words he spoke to me were not just words but more like a command or an assignment.

I was thankful when the day came for me to meet with Pastor Stangel and Karen. I hoped they could ease my mind and help me make sense of the dreams.

27

Purpose and Destiny

"Sometimes when women have experienced the horrific things that you've been through, they still have haunting dreams or flashbacks from their pasts."

"Yes, I know, Pastor. But I'm not in these dreams. They're not about me, yet the girls in my dreams are real. Somehow, I know they're real girls, and they're crying out for my help."

Pastor Stangel leaned forward, his forearms resting on his desk. "Karen and I have prayed about something and have wanted to share it with you for some time now. We put it off considering you and Peter were newlyweds getting to know one another. Then Samantha was born, and you were busy being a new mother. Now God has blessed you with a son, so we know how busy you are. However, we believe God spoke to us that now is the time for us to share something with you."

He glanced at Karen then back at me. "As a pastor I've seen God many times use circumstances we've gone through to enable us to help other people. And God often uses dreams to get a message to us. What starts out as a dream often becomes a nagging at the very essence of our heart. The heinous things you were forced to endure are what give you the desire and compassion to understand and help those women who've gone through much the same things you did."

Tears began to trickle down my cheeks. "Pastor Stangel, is that why I heard this man's voice tell me, 'Yes, Lyndie, you can help them?' Was that God speaking to me?"

"I do believe it was the voice of the Lord," Pastor nodded, "telling you your purpose and destiny."

"It was such a familiar voice," I said, "like the voice of someone I once knew. This is the voice in my quiet times that fills me with total peace."

He grinned. "When God speaks to us and we recognize he's asking us to do something, that's when we find complete rest in him."

A calm assurance filled my heart. "You know something else, Pastor? I'm happier now than I could ever have imagined. I have a husband who adores me. I'm surrounded by a loving family and good friends. God has blessed me with two healthy, beautiful children—yet I feel like there's something more, something like you said, tugging at my heart."

I threw my hands up in frustration. "But how do I help these girls who are victims of sex trafficking? I'm just a young mother. Where do I begin? How and where would I ever be able to get the resources to help them?"

The pastor put up a hand. "Hold on a minute. If this is part of God's plan for your life, He'll provide. All you need to do is trust and obey him. As far as the resources, I think he's already supplied them."

"What do you mean?"

"Do you remember the old farmhouse at the end of the road? The man who owned it died a few years ago, and it's been sitting vacant ever since. Yesterday his family donated it to the church, so there's your start. We'll ask our members to help fix it up. It could be a sanctuary house for girls who have escaped from sex trafficking. This would be your ministry, and through this ministry, you'd be able to fulfill your purpose and destiny. The house has nine bedrooms. We could fix up one of the rooms as a daycare/nursery for your children."

My heart leapt with excitement. "That's it," I clapped. "We could call it The Sanctuary."

"That's perfect whereas the meaning of the word sanctuary is a place of refuge, a safe harbor, and a hideaway. This would be these girls' island sanctuary. Nothing could be better for them than to receive healing on the lovely island of Kauai, one of the most beautiful places in the world, especially after having lived in such ugliness and degradation."

It all sounded so wonderful, and yet ... "Wait a minute. I've never ministered to anyone before, and I don't feel qualified to do this. I don't even know where to begin."

Karen spoke up, her voice gentle but strong. "You of all people know how to reach deep into the souls of these girls more than anyone I know. You've lived the horror they'll be coming out of. God will give you a plan and the right words to say. You need only to trust him. You'll be his hands to these girls."

Encouraged, I nodded, wiping one lone tear from my cheek.

Pastor Stangel cleared his throat, "I've done some extensive research on all this and have compiled a list of ministries in Southern California that work specifically with female survivors of sex trafficking. I'm sure I could phone the directors and schedule a visit for you and Peter to meet with them and tour their facility."

My mouth gaped open. "Oh, my, this is incredible!"

"That's how our Lord works when we're following his plan and purpose for our lives. I think I mentioned this to you before, the things we go through in life are never just for us. They're for the someone else who comes along so we can help them get through something similar. I think today really confirms that for you."

I nodded, the corners of my mouth lifting. I wasn't sure I could contain my excitement long enough to tell Peter all about it.

"Without your pain," Pastor said, "you'd not be equipped to have this wonderful ministry God has called you into. In the book of Isaiah, the Lord promises to give us 'beauty for ashes.'"

It was all beginning to make sense to me, and my heart raced with anticipation.

The pastor continued, "God is going to pick you up from the ashes and make something beautiful out of your life. His body was broken so our lives could be put back together. What the Lord did in your life, God will help you do for others."

Wow, me help other girls! Oh, God, can I really do that?

Deep within my heart I heard a soft voice: *Don't be afraid. Remember where your help comes from.*

⇜28⇝

The Sanctuary

The following week Peter and I flew to Los Angeles to visit some residential programs for sex-trafficked women. The grandparents were overjoyed to care for their grandkids for a week, and we knew they couldn't be in more loving hands.

While in Los Angeles we visited three facilities. The first one was called Grandma's House of Hope. We learned from the director that the sale of humans is the second largest illegal industry worldwide, right behind the sale of guns and drug trafficking. Another facility was called Breaking the Chains. The premise was to provide healing and restoration to survivors of sex trafficking. Both ministries worked with local, state, and federal law enforcement agencies to provide rescue, relocation, restoration, and residential services to adult victims of human trafficking.

The facility I liked most was Redeeming Love. Their mission statement? Every life is created to be free and experience Redeeming Love. They provide a safe and nurturing home for young women seeking rehabilitation from sex trafficking. The organization supported the survivors through the process of restoration, their goal being to help them discover how every past could be redeemed, repurposed, and made new. Charlene Heydorn, the founder, offered to help us with whatever we needed to get started.

Redeeming Love only accepted women eighteen or older into their program. This determination was based on the belief that younger girls would be able to return to their families and get the help and love they needed at home. Peter and I decided we would take any age girl. I understood how hard it was to return home without being restored by Christ.

Redeeming Love's program consisted of trauma therapy, life assistance, and mentoring. Charlene believed at the epicenter of recovery from sex trafficking is the recovery of the heart. Trauma-trained therapists worked closely with each survivor to bring healing and integration to mind, body, heart, and spirit. The second aspect of the program was life assistance. With healing of the heart in motion, they worked on necessary life skills, job readiness, and job placement, along with education completion and career counseling. The last part of their program was mentoring to help every woman recognize they were created with a God-given purpose. Christian mentors worked with the survivors on their journey to discovering their unique purpose in this world.

Peter and I learned a great deal and met such wonderful, knowledgeable people during our time in California. Yet on the plane trip home, I felt somewhat overwhelmed and insufficient. I wasn't a trained therapist, nor did we have the financial resources to provide for these girls' needs.

When I brought up my concerns to Peter about our inability to supply all we needed to start a home, he assured me, "God will provide. This is his ministry. Our inability is his ability. Trust him."

I brushed my lips against Peter's warm cheek. "I don't deserve you."

Peter pulled me into his arms and gently kissed my lips, sending my stomach into a wild swirl.

When Kimo picked us up at the airport, he had one of the silliest grins I'd ever seen. When we asked him what was up, he shrugged, "You'll see."

My dad was the one who broke the amazing news to us. Businesses in the community, which Sam and the Stangels had contacted, responded to our needs to start The Sanctuary. Three furniture stores donated bedroom furnishings for eight bedrooms. Sears took care of the furniture for the nursery/daycare. Costco Warehouse gave us furniture for the living room and office space, and one of Peter's aunts gave us her barn-style dining room table and benches.

My parents stocked the kitchen cabinets with the prettiest dishes and all the pots and pans and gadgets we could ever imagine. A local paint company brought over a crew to paint the inside and outside of the farmhouse.

When Noelani wasn't busy sewing curtains for the windows, she was putting fresh flowers in the vases she'd placed in each room. I hadn't even realized that this farmhouse came with a beautiful garden of flowers, but Noelani used them to make the whole place look cheery. Sam, Kimo, and my dad sanded and varnished the vintage wood floors.

One day when Peter and I were walking around The Sanctuary grounds, we ran into Pastor Stangel. "More than $250,000 and a minivan have been donated to The Sanctuary," he gushed. "In addition, several people have made monthly pledges, and Karen has put together a board to oversee the ministry."

"Wow, when God moves, he moves fast," I said.

One Sunday, a woman named Mary Lou Simpson, one of the older ladies in the congregation, approached me after church. "I'm extremely excited about you opening up The Sanctuary. I'm a retired licensed counselor, and I'd love to be a part of all this. Of course, this is strictly as a volunteer. I don't want nor would I accept any salary. I know I'll receive much more from the Lord for helping than any money could buy. I just want to be able to be a part of these young girls' recovery."

"Oh, my, Mary Lou," I said, as tears filled eyes, "you are such an answer to prayer."

Sam also got involved, handcrafting and hanging wooden plaques with inspirational scriptures on the walls of the farmhouse. We wanted the girls who passed through the rooms to see we have a God who loves us and will provide for us in all areas of our life, and he is still in the business of making something beautiful out of our brokenness. Sam hung a plague with my favorite scripture from Isaiah 53 in the living room, where it serves as a prayer for healing for these young girls:

Surely he took our pain and bore our suffering, yet we considered him punished by God, stricken by him, and afflicted. But he was pierced for our transgressions, he was crushed for our iniquities; the punishment that brought us peace was on him, and by his wounds we are healed.

All of us involved wanted these girls to see God as the God of love and healing. He is an all-knowing God, the One who knows and can relate to our deepest fear and pain. He is the Healer who has the ability to grant peace when no one else can and who, despite the horror and darkness we've been through, can offer hope that outweighs all the brokenness we've experienced. Since these girls' deepest need is to be whole, redeemed, and restored, we wanted to point them to the One whose love can do just that.

As God sent the girls to The Sanctuary, it was my own pain and brokenness that strengthened and equipped me to relate to and minister to them. The Word of God and the love of all the workers helped bring healing to the hearts and minds of those we were fortunate to be able to minister to at The Sanctuary.

We had three to five girls, ages ranging from twelve to eighteen, living in the home at the same time. Each time a girl was ready to leave our program, we held a gala celebration. Sam was the master of ceremonies. The girls adored him and called him Papa Sam. He took every girl's plight to heart just as he did mine. You could often find Sam taking extra special time talking, witnessing, and loving each girl individually, quickly becoming their best friend. Tears often flowed at the ceremonies—mostly tears of happiness.

During their stay at The Sanctuary, one requirement of the girls was to keep a freedom journal, in which they documented how God was molding them into something beautiful. At the ceremony we required them all to share something from the journal that was significant in their personal road to restoration. Sometimes it was just a scripture that spoke to them, but many times it was a song or a poem the Lord had given them in their quiet time. These were all copied and added to The Sanctuary's "big book," along with pictures of the girls who'd written them beside their entries.

The more the girls studied God's Word and stayed in his presence, the stronger they became. Pastor Stangel and his wife also involved themselves with the program. Karen and Mrs. Simpson encouraged and counseled each girl, while Pastor Stangel held a weekly Bible study for them. In experiencing the unconditional love of Christ, they were able to begin loving themselves and others. God was at work restoring their lives, and they were getting their stolen joy back.

Char Lin, a Japanese American with long black hair, almond-shaped eyes, and porcelain skin, was the first girl to stay at The Sanctuary. She was as delicate as she was beautiful. Mom and I sat down with her when she arrived.

"We want your stay here to be safe and comfortable," I said. "You don't have to share anything with us that you don't want to."

Smiling shyly, she said, "Thank you, Ms. Lyndie. I would like to tell you what happened to me."

"Okay. We're here to listen and help."

"I was thirteen years old when I was walking home from a convenience store. A van pulled alongside, and a man jumped out and grabbed me, then dragged me inside. They drugged me. I came to hours later and found myself in an old, abandoned animal shelter. Fifteen other girls were held captive there too. We were put into groups of four, then they put each group into large animal cages."

I put my hand on Char Lin's, aching with the fear and pain she must have felt.

"At night they released us at gunpoint," she continued. "We were forced to shower, dress, and make ourselves up. Then, again in groups of four, they took us out for street prostitution. Only if we returned with the required amount of money would they feed us. If not, we were beaten. Escape was not a possibility, as the pimps kept a watchful eye on us. When one girl tried to escape, she was caught and tortured with a cigarette lighter in front of us. No one tried to escape again."

Carol, the next girl to come to stay at The Sanctuary, was only fourteen. She was petite with red hair and freckles and looked like she could have been a cheerleader. She and Char Lin immediately became buddies. We soon discovered that Carol was blessed with a beautiful singing voice. During one of our meetings after Friday chapel she said, "Could Char Lin and I do worship?"

I was thrilled to see Carol had befriended Char Lin. "Yes, of course."

"Ms. Lyndie," Char Lin said, "Carol has written a wonderful song called 'He Can Put You Back Together.'"

"I'd love to hear you girls sing that at our next chapel," Mom said, "and I'd enjoy teaching you girls some other worship songs. I think you'd really like Bill Gaither's song 'Something Beautiful.'"

"Sure, Mom," the girls chimed in together, referring to my mother as "Mom," something they had started doing soon after meeting her.

As it turned out, Carol's song became the theme song for The Sanctuary.

Lori was the next girl to become part of The Sanctuary. Lori was tall and slim. She had a natural beauty with sun-streaked hair and big brown eyes. We soon learned that she was a talented artist.

One evening when we were all sitting around the living room, Sam asked the girls, "Tomorrow I'm going into town for supplies. Is there anything you'd like me to get for you while I'm there?"

Lori spoke up first. "Could you please get me some canvases and watercolors?"

"I would be happy if you could find some origami paper for me," said Char Lin.

"What's origami?" asked Carol.

"I'll explain and show you how to make things when I get the paper," Char Lin replied.

"Can I have some Pistachio nuts?" Carol giggled.

"I'll do my best, girls."

"Thank you, Papa Sam," they echoed together.

As soon as Lori received her supplies, she started painting.

Our counselor, Mary Lou, confided in me, "Lori expresses the pain from the things she was put through during her abduction in her paintings. It has become a way of release for her. You must come and see her latest watercolor."

"Let's go have a look."

I gasped when I saw what she had painted. It was a young girl with bad memories replaying in her head. She illustrated this by showing each time a negative thought tried to replay in the girl's mind, she'd tie a balloon around it and send it off to heaven. Underneath the picture she wrote in calligraphy:

We demolish arguments and every pretension that sets itself up against the knowledge of God, and we take captive every thought to make it obedient to Christ
(2 Corinthians 10:5).

Char Lin and Carol came to see the painting.

"That's amazing!" Char Lin said.

"You should be a professional artist," said Carol.

"Your painting is lovely. Can we hang it up in the living room?" I asked.

Her eyes sparkled. "Sure, Ms. Lyndie."

Jennifer and Elaine showed up the same week. The girls welcomed them with hugs. Jennifer was a shy little girl with a kind heart and a love for animals. She had long, curly blonde hair and deep-set blue eyes.

One day she asked Char Lin, "Is there an animal shelter on the island?'

"I'm not sure. I'll ask Papa Sam."

Sam said there was.

When Jennifer saw Sam the next day, she asked, "Can you take us for a visit to the animal shelter?"

"Of course," he replied. "That sounds like fun."

When they arrived at the animal shelter, the owner asked Jennifer, "Would you like to volunteer here on Saturdays?'

Her eyes lit up. "Oh, could I really? What do you think, Papa Sam?"

"You'll have to get permission from Ms. Lyndie," he cautioned. "But I'm certain she'll agree to it."

The people who ran the shelter loved Jennifer, and she was a hard worker. One day, someone left a litter of puppies at the shelter. The puppies looked like they were border collies. Jennifer helped take care of the runt, and the director asked if she would like to take it back to The Sanctuary. She readily accepted, and the love and companionship of our pet dog, Hope, helped tremendously in each girl's healing.

Jennifer came home one Saturday with exciting news. "The North Shore Veterinarian Clinic owner came into the shelter today and asked me if I'd like to work part-time as a veterinarian assistant."

"Wow, that's great news!" I said.

"That's not all. He said if I did good, he'd scholarship me to obtain certification as a vet tech."

I could see God was opening doors for these girls to transition back into a normal life.

Elaine soon became Jennifer's closest friend. She had a bubbly personality that matched her short pixie-cut brown hair and green eyes. Elaine loved to write, using it to push through her pain. After supper, the girls would all sit around in the living room and chat. One evening, Mom and I walked into the room and heard lots of excitement.

"What is it, girls?" I asked.

"You have to hear this," said Jennifer. "Elaine wrote the most awesome poem."

I couldn't wait to hear it. "Would you share it with us?"

Elaine read her poem aloud:

Broken Is Beautiful

Broken fragments can always be mended. Just as the Lord took all the pieces of my shattered life and refitted them back together into something beautiful, useful, and worthy, he can do the same thing with the broken pieces of your life.

You need only to place the broken, wounded pieces of your heart into the hand of our loving Father. You need to be broken at the feet of Jesus. Let him deal with those who caused you so much pain.

Something will change inside of you, and healing will begin when you stop looking inward and start looking upward.

Jesus' body was broken for you, but God put him back together into a glorified body, he will put you back together into something beautiful.

You will go from victim to rescuer, and from fearful to courageous. God will use your brokenness to help someone else.

"That is so beautiful," my mother exclaimed. "I really think when you leave here and go home, you should pursue a career as a writer."

"You really think so, Mom?"

"I do."

Carol spoke up then. "Look what Char Lin taught me to make today." She held up a perfectly folded paper crane.

"Will you teach us how to make one too?" asked Lori.

"Yes," said Char Lin, "but first I want to tell you a story. I told this story to the other girls I was held captive with. I thought I could bring them some hope.

Sadako Sasaki lived in Hiroshima at the time the United States dropped the atom bomb on her city. Although she was only two years old when the bomb was dropped, at twelve years old she was diagnosed with leukemia [an atom bomb related disease] from the radiation. She was given a year to live. Her friends told her of the Japanese legend—the person who creates a thousand origami cranes will be granted a wish. She was inspired by the legend to fold paper cranes in the hope of making a thousand. Sadako's wish was simply to live. Sadly, she folded only six hundred forty-four cranes before she became too weak to fold anymore. Her friends and family finished her dream by folding the rest of the cranes, which were buried with Sadako. My story ended sadly, but it gave hope to the girls I told it to.

"While in captivity, we picked up scraps of paper everywhere we went. I taught them how to fold origami paper cranes. Our captors allowed us to fold the cranes since it kept us calm and quiet. Our goal was to fold one thousand cranes. One of the girls came up with the idea, every time one of them finished a crane, they'd say a little prayer and send it up to heaven. Of course, we all prayed to be rescued. One night, the police raided the compound. We hadn't folded one thousand cranes, but our prayers were answered."

"What a wonderful story," said Carol. "Teach us how to make the paper cranes so we can fold one thousand and pray for girls who still need to be rescued."

When Char Lin came to The Sanctuary, Sam told her about

God's love for her, and she gave her heart to Jesus. She showed her thankfulness to him by continuing to fold the cranes and offering up prayers for other unknown girls in the world of sex trafficking. She taught origami to every girl who came after her. Those cranes now decorate the living room of The Sanctuary.

The girls stayed in touch with us and with one another after they left The Sanctuary and went home. Char Lin called shortly after being reunited with her family.

"Ms. Lyndie," she said, "I miss you all. I thank you for teaching me to pray whenever I get fearful. My folks have been so loving, just as you assured me they would."

My heart swelled with joy. "And we miss you. Our new girls are learning origami too."

"That's wonderful! You know, I'm in junior college now and want to become a counselor."

"I think you will make a very fine counselor," I assured her.

"Thank you. I'll keep in touch and let you know how I'm doing."

"Yes, please do. We love you, Char."

It wasn't long after Carol left, we received a letter from her parents.

Dear Ms. Lyndie & Staff,

We want you to know the time we came to visit Carol at The Sanctuary and the day we picked her up we felt nothing but love from you all. We agree the time our daughter spent there helped her make an easier transition back to our home. Carol is singing on the worship team at church. Although she is still not able to open up with us about what she went through, the counselor she is seeing is helping her cope with the occasional nightmares. We will never forget what you did for our daughter. She loved Sam. She said he always made time to listen. We will continue to support you in prayer and financially.

—*Mr. and Mrs. Able*

Lori often sent us photos of her paintings, and she would write little notes on the back of each photo. We could see she was still working through her healing process within her artwork. On one particular painting she had painted of a young girl laying her backpack at the foot of the Cross she wrote: "Laying burdens down never to pick up again."

We were thrilled to receive an invitation to Jennifer's wedding. She had returned home to Colorado Springs with her certification as a veterinarian technician and got a job at an animal hospital. Not long after, a young man named Jim, just out of veterinary school, joined the team at the hospital. He and Jennifer began to attend church together, and a year later, they became engaged. Jim sounded like a wonderful man for her. Mom, Sam, and I made plans to attend the wedding.

Elaine was the girl who surprised us the most. Of all those who went through the program at The Sanctuary, she had the most problem reintegrating, experiencing feelings of social alienation.

One day Elaine phoned, "How do I communicate with people now? I've missed all the milestones of growing up in a loving environment. I never got to be a teenager."

Mom talked to her and tried to encourage her. "Take one day at a time," she advised.

We didn't hear back from Elaine for a while but continued to pray for her until she called again.

"Not long after I talked to you, I was watching a program on sex trafficking," she said. "The commentator kept referring to the girls as victims. This caused a lot of emotions to rise in me, especially anger. I was no longer a victim. I was a survivor! So, I decided to get involved to help raise awareness about the hidden signs of sex trafficking. I felt a need to speak out in my community. Now my story is being told on news outlets and college campuses. My book is almost finished. Thank you for being there for me."

"We believed in you all along," I told her, "and knew there was greatness in you, Elaine."

Every time I say goodbye to one of my girls, I think back to the young girl—me—who wanted to help little Suzi not have to live as a sex slave and endure the loss of her innocence through abuse, drugs, rape, or prostitution. I thank God for giving me the strength and courage to escape and to help free Suzi.

As for dealing with my captors, at first it was difficult to forgive them and even harder to pray for them. Then, during my prayer time, the Lord spoke to me and gave me a glimpse of himself on the cross. He told me he died for my captors too. He showed me how much he loves them and desires all to be saved. I realized the forgiveness I needed to give wasn't for them but for me. In forgiving them, I found freedom.

≈29≈

The Wedding

Suzi patted my shoulder. I turned around and gave her a hug. Sweet Suzi, so strong and confident, not the little puppy-dog-eyed girl looking to me for help. She'd even written and published a book about my life. *Restored ... Saving One Life at a Time.* It sold a good number of copies and helped raise awareness that sex trafficking is not just a third-world issue.

"I'm so glad Peter hired a detective to find you and reunite us," I said.

"Yes, dear Lyndie," her eyes glistening with tears, "I remember how I fell in love with Kauai, moved here, and now you're my best friend. God truly had a plan in all this. I can't thank you enough for the opportunity to be the new administrator of The Sanctuary."

"You are more than capable," I assured her.

"I'm in the process of writing a proposal to open two other Sanctuaries, one on Oahu and one on Maui."

"Sounds terrific!" I turned toward the front when the music started playing.

The opening song, "When God Made You," brought tears of joy down my cheeks. I thought of how special it was for my precious daughter, Samantha, to choose the same song Peter and I chose for our own wedding.

I overheard a woman in the pew behind me whisper, "She's perfectly lovely. That dress is stunning on her." The woman next to her whispered back, "It's even more stunning on her sleek body and with what's no doubt her year-around tan."

Satin and lace rustled softly beside me. What a beautiful

bride my daughter was. Auburn curls fell long to her shoulders. And then she stopped and turned toward me. Her eyes met mine, and she blessed me with one of her radiant, sweet smiles that seemed to paint a ray of sunshine all over her face. She mouthed, "Thanks, Mom," as her jade, almond-shaped eyes sparkled.

Standing there at my daughter's wedding, I reflected on what a blessing she was from the Lord. A wave of melancholy washed over me, as I thought of the place she would leave vacant in our home and in my heart. I overflowed with love and happiness for her. Today Samantha was marrying the man of her dreams, Ronnie Edwards. They met while she was at the University of Hawaii studying nursing. He was in his first year of residency as a pediatrician. They fell in love instantly on the night they met, much the way Peter and I had done. Ronnie told her on their first date he would marry her someday, though Samantha told him he was out of his mind. It wasn't long before she realized he was right.

Now Ronnie's face beamed as he saw Samantha approaching on her father's arm. Peter turned his gaze towards me, winked, and smiled. "I love you," he whispered. After all these years and all we'd been through, I still tingled when Peter's eyes met mine. He's my man, and my man alone. His smile still thrilled me, much as it had when we first met on the flight to Honolulu. That day was the beginning of my journey from the world of nightmarish demoralization to a land of peaceful paradise. What a strikingly handsome man Peter is! Admiring his broad shoulders, the lock of wavy hair falling toward his eye, his captivating smile, I fell in love with him all over again.

Of all the people in the wedding party, my dear son, Caleb, seemed to stand out the most. He was simply adorable with a tangled mop of blond hair, his charming dimples, and his childishly innocent aquamarine eyes. I marveled at how proud I was of my little man—though he wasn't so little anymore. He had such a gentle and quiet spirit, yet he loved and excelled at sports. It was only his third year of high school, and already a major-league recruiter had scouted him.

A tight squeeze of my hand by Sam brought me back to the moment. Dear Sam. I looked up at the man who had rescued me—not just physically but more importantly, spiritually. I fervently believe his faith in God and his prayers were largely responsible for bringing me to where I was. Sam didn't move as quickly as he once did. In all my life, I'd never met a kinder or sweeter soul, so full of love and joy, and he readily spread love and joy to everyone he met. It seemed he always had a smile on his face and a kind word for everyone. The only time I saw Sam sad was when his beloved dog and companion, Sandy, passed away.

Glancing across the pews at Peter's parents, Noelani and Kimo, I realize I couldn't have dreamed of having such devoted relatives. Not only were they by my side physically when Peter left years earlier, but they'd covered me in prayer daily ever since. They always helped me with whatever I needed. Noelani and Kimo were also the most loving grandparents our children could ever have. Both jumped right in when I started The Sanctuary, helping and supporting me in every way possible.

My mom, sitting on the other side of me, touched my hand, smiled, and whispered, "You did well, Lyndie." I thought back to the unspeakable pain she and my father had to endure when I was kidnapped. Yet my mom had remained strong in her faith and never lost hope. Nor did she stop believing God would bring me safely home. Even though she missed out on years of mothering me, God in his loving grace and mercy allowed her to mother over forty girls at The Sanctuary. Many times, she rushed up to me with cards and letters addressed to Mom from girls who'd graduated from the program.

My mother treated each girl like her own daughter and, in

turn, they gave her the title Mom. Their letters always contained a message thanking her for helping and loving them. God truly restored the missed years to my mom just like the scripture tells us, "And I will restore to you the years that the swarming locust has eaten, the hopper, the destroyer, and the cutter, my great army, which I sent among you."

Smiling, she said, "God has richly blessed you. He has truly given you beauty for ashes."

I nodded and closed my eyes, silently thanking God for all he'd done in my life. The singer interrupted my thoughts with strains of "Because He Lives." I took a deep breath, remembering how that song sustained me each time the enemy tried to flash in my mind reruns of a tiny room with its filthy mattress where innocence was shattered. My grandmother had taught me the words. Like a lifeline, I sang them in my head during my time in bondage. Let them settle in my head even now.

Because He lives, I can face tomorrow.

Afterword

It's been more than fifteen years since we started The Sanctuary, and we've seen forty-three girls rescued and returned free and whole to their families. Free to live a life full of hope, grace, and love. They are redeemed, restored, set free, and serving God.

I saw healing continue over the years, as many of the girls stayed on for a while to become a big sister and mentor to the new arrivals. What a privilege to be used of God and witness him taking these girls who came to us broken, fearful, and full of shame, and then transforming them to victorious, free, and forgiven daughters of the King. They were no longer slaves of their past but could now stand complete in him.

I've learned victims of human trafficking can be so conditioned by their captors, that all self-worth and free will are stripped away, and they believe the lie: they were willing participants in the evil in which they were ensnared. The fear of being tortured, starved, or even killed, paralyzes them. The repeated forced drugging, along with the threat of harm to their family members, immobilizes them. They simply exist, and life happens to them. They believe they have no power or ability to control or change their circumstances. It is only through the power of the Cross and the blood of Jesus Christ that these girls can find their true identity in him and get their lives back.

My life is a lot like the 500-year-old Japanese art of *Kintsugi* or "golden journey." It's the method of restoring broken pieces of pottery with a lacquer mixed with gold, silver, or platinum. I was broken. God was the glue. He must have seen something beautiful in me when he reassembled the shattered pieces of my life and fused them together, not with precious metals, but with love, forgiveness, and grace. I once found this promise in Revelation 21:4. I hold on to it to give me hope.

He will wipe every tear from their eyes. There will be no more death or mourning or crying or pain, for the old order of things has passed away.

This is my story. And this is God's goodness.

Discussion Questions

1   What does the Bible say about restoration? How was Lyndie restored? What things in your life has God restored?

2   Peter and Lyndie experienced problems in their marriage due to Lyndie's past. What could they have each done differently to avoid these problems? Explain how Lyndie was able to give her heart totally to Peter.

3   Fear not only crippled Lyndie, but it left her hopeless. What did she do to conquer that fear? Is there a time in your own life when you lived in fear?

4   What circumstances surrounded Lyndie, enabling her to become convinced of Christ's love for her? What situations in your life convinced you of God's love for you?

5   How did Lyndie's plight emotionally impact you? What impacted you most?

6   How did reading this book affect your thoughts about human trafficking?

7   After reading this book, are you motivated to learn more about trafficking or to get involved in the fight against this modern-day slavery?

8   Pastor Stangel and his wife, Karen, played a significant role in Lyndie and Peter's lives. Describe the positive influence they had on the couple's relationship. In what ways has a pastor influenced your relationships in any way?

9   How did God use Sam in Lyndie's life? In what ways did Lyndie impact Sam?

10 Lyndie had two voices speaking in her head throughout the story—God and Satan. Have you ever felt God was speaking to you? Satan? How can you distinguish between the two voices?

11 At Lyndie's daughter's wedding, Lyndie's mom says to Lyndie, "You did well." What do you think she meant? What effect do you think those words had on Lyndie? Was there a time in your life when someone spoke positive words that impacted you?

12 There is always purpose in our pain. It is often said that things don't just happen to you just for you, but also for someone else. How does this hold true in Lyndie's life? Has this happened in your life?

13 Violence, abuse, and sexual slavery are not usual subjects in Christian novels. Were you comfortable with how the author handled these topics?

14 Were you surprised that fear drove Lyndie to avoid going home to her family and instead got on a plane to Hawaii? Can you remember a time that you were driven by fear and made a poor choice?

15 How did Lyndie find true freedom? What are some of the steps that brought freedom and healing to Lyndie?

16 Someone once said that unforgiveness is like drinking poison and waiting for the other person to die. What does the Bible say about forgiveness? How was Lyndie forgiving her abductors important to her healing? Is there someone in your life you need to forgive?

17 Lyndie desired so much to be liked and accepted by Anthony she ignored her mother's warning and found herself thrust into the heinous world of human trafficking. Have you ever ignored a warning and then found yourself in an inescapable predicament?

18 Ruth Johnson, Lyndie's mom, had relentless faith in her daughter's imminent return even when her husband Steve lost hope. How did God reward Ruth's faith?

19 Fiction can teach and touch your heart. What did you glean

from this book? In what way did it touch your heart, change, or enlighten you?

20 The things that happened to Lyndie were horrific. These things are happening today in real life. Many of us wonder where God is and why he doesn't intervene. Have you wondered why horrible things happen to innocent children? Where is God in these situations?

21 Total surrender opens the door for God's restoration. In the Afterword, the author compares Lyndie's life to the art of Kintsugi, the method of taking broken pieces of pottery and restoring them with precious metals. What things need restoration in your life?

22 How does trusting in God's plan change your life?

About the Author

DEJAH EDWARDS is an inspirational author and speaker. She has earned a Masters degree in biblical counseling and education. She is the author of the nonfiction books *Mama I Want To Be Like You, Honor Yourself You Are Highly Favored and Loved,* and *God's Lent Child.* Her passion is to bring hope and healing to women through her writing. Dejah, her husband, Ron, and their two dogs live in Yucaipa, California.

Contact Information

Dejah Edwards would love to hear from her readers. If you would like to send a comment, contact her to book a speaking engagement, or to order more copies of this book,

email her at Dejah05@gmail.com
or you can visit her website
www.deeplylovedbyHim.com